# Yule Be Home For Solstice

Sharon K. Angelici

Cover Art by Taylor Rose

First Edition



Write with Light Publications
Colorado, USA

ISBN: 978-1-7378158-5-3
Library of Congress Number: 2023948996

# Dedication

For my husband, my daughter and my son. You inspire me and I'm grateful for the minutes, days and years of living this adventure called life. I'm glad you are mine.

For my Aussie family, including our rescued greyhound fur babies. I cannot imagine my life without you in it. Your courage led me to find my own. We have done incredible things with all this love.

To my Minnesota family and support team, I love you all so very much and those early beta reads get me through. Much love to you all, always.

To Dad, thanks for reading my books even if they aren't your cup of tea.

To my mother, my fiction writing begins and ends because you inspired me to be more. Even after your heart stopped beating, and the days felt impossible, you made me believe. If wishes were reality you'd be holding this book in your beautiful hands drinking a cup of tea with me.

# CHAPTER ONE

"Phone's ringing!" Alice tossed her backpack on the table as she stomped her snow-covered boots on the kitchen rug. She listened for an answer but the modest, ranch-style house was quiet. "Honey, your phone is ringing," she called again, tugging her hat off to release the freshly-shaved undercut. The season of winter solstice was upon them, this winter celebration was her second favorite holiday next to Imbolc's fire festival, she had to admit she was excited. "Violet, your phone is ringing."

"I can hear it." Violet popped out of the bathroom, a towel knotted over her curvaceous body. Her graying long black hair hung dripping a puddle by her feet. "I'm kinda…" She waved her hand up and down in front of her torso.

"Kinda delicious." Alice took a step toward her wife of twenty years.

"Stop." Violet let go of the towel to hold a halting palm up. "Snowy and wet boots!"

Alice picked up the phone. "You should answer it." She held it behind her back.

"Alice." Violet's tone was scolding but playful as she clenched the towel.

"Oh shit, we should answer it." The word 'Auntie' and a photo of the older woman's smiling face filled the screen.

"Uh, yeah." Violet dashed toward the bedroom.

"Hello, Eunice," Alice said as she hit the speaker option on the phone.

"Hello, my dear." Violet's aunt's voice was hushed with a scratchy vibration typical of her enthusiastic chanting and tendency towards excessive conversation.

"How are you?" Alice bent to untie her boot laces.

"I'm a little tired. That's why I'm calling. I need to talk to the two of you about our solstice celebration."

"What's going on?" Violet stepped out of the bedroom with a t-shirt clinging to her wet body. She took the phone from her wife and they stood together in their kitchen.

"I've overextended myself this year and don't think we can do our Yule log."

"What?" they said in unison. The celebration was tradition; for the past nearly twenty years the two of them had sat beside Violet's aunt to celebrate the shift from darkness to light.

"The harvest. I didn't harvest the aspen."

Alice waved at her wife and whispered, "We can get an aspen log."

Violet nodded. She opened the messaging app on her laptop and clicked the name of their good friend Jackson. With nimble fingers, Violet typed out a message, multi-tasking as she continued to listen to the woman on the other end of the phone. "Auntie, we don't want to cancel. We'll get the tree."

**Violet:** need oak or aspen tree. What you got?"
**Jackson:** limbs down at the cabin
**Violet:** oak or aspen?
**Jackson:** aspen
**Violet:** perfect

"If you're sure it won't be a bother? I know it's very last minute." Aunt Eunice's voice sounded hoarse, a little fatigued for the normally energetic family matriarch. Seasonal transitions were usually her time to shine and the request worried Violet. She decided on the spot that she would do whatever was necessary to take care of her aunt.

**Jackson:** when are you coming? I'm packing up to leave the cabin for solstice.
**Violet:** tomorrow???

Violet made a thumbs-up gesture at Alice.

"No, it won't be a bother at all, Auntie. Remember, Alice and I met on a hiking trip and she loves any chance to trek in the woods." Her brown eyes blinked hard as she focused on the computer screen.

**Jackson:** I'll tie a red ribbon around the limb. festive just for you.
**Violet:** not a yellow ribbon??? Lol
**Jackson:** it's not an oak tree. LOL
**Violet:** thanks Jackson
**Jackson:** np, bring a saw
**Violet:** will do
**Jackson:** maybe snowshoes too because we're supposed to get a few inches of snow tonight

"Super," she thought as she stared at the last line in the messaging window. She was not excited to trek through snow.

"You understand all of the requirements?" Her aunt's question would have been insulting if Violet didn't understand the importance of their Yule celebration.

"I know the rules and restrictions. It's almost as if you've been telling them to me for forty years." Violet stifled her giggle.

"Always a smarty-pants," her aunt scolded. "So it's settled, you're taking charge."

Violet nodded, even though her aunt couldn't see her. "Yes, Auntie, we've got everything under control." She hit the exit button on her message pinning all her hopes on that aspen limb and Jackson's ability to mark it so they could find it.

~~~~~~~~~~~

"The driveway isn't plowed," Alice said, as she estimated where to turn into the driveway.

"Jackson said it was going to snow." Violet squeaked out her reminder.

"All-wheel drive it is." Alice could make out the remnants of the last snowstorm's plow lumps along both sides of the nearly mile-long driveway. "It's a good thing Jackson likes his big-boy toys." She was confident in her car's ability to make it to the cabin.

"He also said to bring snowshoes. Oh shit. I forgot to tell you that."

Alice rolled down the window, enjoying the strange wave of heat at thirty-two degrees following the storm. "I didn't bring snowshoes, Vi."

"Jackson has some. We've used them before."
~~~~~~~~~~~

Alice walked around the cabin to the shed. She keyed the door open but the snowshoes were not hanging in their spot. "Shit!" She whispered, knowing what was ahead as she rounded the cabin empty-handed.

"No shoes?"

"No shoes, my love."

Violet shrugged. "How deep could it be?"

It was absolutely the wrong question to ask after they took the first steps off the unshoveled walkway.

"If this snow gets any deeper, I'm going to pinch you and Aunt Eunice when I see her." Alice's six-foot frame sunk inches deeper into the knee-high snow. The two of them were on a mission to find a single fallen tree in a snow-covered forest. How hard could it be? Alice's crinkling thermal pants hung snuggly over her shoulders but her feet were warm in the treaded boots cinched tight to lock out the snow. If she knew anything, it was how to stay warm in the wilderness. Snowshoes would have been helpful, though.

"You do realize that pinching a witch might not be a good idea." Violet was nearly a foot shorter than her wife and curvy where Alice was not. She giggled as most of her leg disappeared into a particularly deep footstep left behind by Alice's size-ten boots.

"Maybe pinching a witch is dangerous, but she had months to pass this Yule baton." Alice grunted as she sidestepped icicle-covered piles of brush and tree rubble, holding them so her wife didn't get slapped in the face.

They were in a forest, surrounded by trees, but none of them were aspens and there wasn't a red ribbon in sight. Her enthusiasm waned as they trekked deeper to retrieve the fallen limb. She wasn't out of shape; in fact, she felt just like the adventurer who met Violet twenty years earlier. It was the chill of winter she didn't miss. The chill wasn't going to stop her, though, as she'd do anything to make the solstice celebration perfect, even if it meant schlepping knee deep through fresh-fallen snow with inadequate footwear.

Violet thought about her aunt. The woman was a witch by history's standards but to her she was an earth-loving human – the type of crone that Alice wished to be one day. Her wife made a great point; collecting fallen tree limbs would have been so much easier on an autumn day. "You're right."

The crunching of boots alternating through soft and hard snow fell silent. "Wait, what?" Alice turned to look at her wife, forcing the short, full-figured woman to bump against her and into her arms. Alice dropped the pruning saw to cradle her wife, preventing the two of them from toppling over.

"Oh, just stop." Violet smirked. "You can be right once in a while." She hopped over, smashed a kiss on Alice's lips and pushed at her solid shoulders.

"I'll remind you later that you said that." Alice turned, picked up the saw and pointed it toward the forest. "Remind me again what Jackson's text said?"

"He said that there was an aspen down on the property and he would come out and tie a festive red ribbon on it."

"Did you think to ask him how far from the cabin, where we parked our car," she emphasized the parking part of the trek, "this festive, red-ribboned aspen was located?"

Violet chuckled. "I forgot the cabin was on so many acres, so no, and Auntie said the Yule wood we burn requires very specific acquisition." She counted on her glove-covered fingers. "We have to find it in the wild. We have to claim it for celebratory purposes, and…" she paused for dramatic effect.

Alice finished, "Under no circumstances can anyone profit from the collection of the Yule celebratory wood."

Violet wriggled her three fingers, converting them into a floating wave to scoot her wife forward. "So move it along, beautiful."

They hiked deeper, weaving through what would have been a delightful pocket of wildflowers a few months ago, but was now mostly matted tangles of stems making little domes in the snow.

"Honey." Alice stopped when her hat snagged on the branch of a pine tree. She felt the chill as the December temperatures of the American Northwest hit the buzz-shaved undercut on the back of her uncovered head.

"Yes, love." Violet laughed as she snatched the hat from the branch.

"Eunice did this to us on purpose, you know?"

Violet grinned. "Auntie loves you and she's turning seventy. She doesn't need to trek through the woods anymore. Not when she has the burliest in-law, who grew up in the wild, to do it for her."

Alice turned to retrieve the hat and found Violet there, her hard-working fingers opening the stocking cap wide enough to pull it onto her wife's head. "I didn't grow up in the wild." She pouted.

Violet smiled. "We practically met in the wild, and back then, everything you owned fit in a backpack, so I'm calling it exactly as we lived it."

"Those were some really great times." Alice thought about her life as a free-spirited and solitary wilderness survival guide with the ability to move around the country and exist with no strings tying her down. She also remembered her level of fitness, which had piqued the curiosity of the woman in front of her. She cherished the knowledge that her wife could read her so easily, but it also frustrated her during moments like this. "I know you only love me for my burl." Alice poked fun as she tucked the longer, untied front strands of her hair beneath the hat.

"Hon, you're so adorable when you pout." Violet strummed her wife's protruding lip. "And after twenty years, you should know that your burl is why I stay."

The wink that followed was Alice's weakness. When Vi turned that smile on her, and the dimples appeared with that wink, it was all she could do to reel in the thrumming feeling deep in her body, even after the highs and lows of their life together. "You're only saying that because you want me and my burliness to carry Aunt Eunice's aspen limbs back the way we came."

"You bet your ass I do." Violet wiped her hands clean of the task. "And if you'd turn your whiny butt around, you'd see the red ribbon on the tree limb right over there." Violet ducked under her wife's arm to point at the tree. It was obnoxious and charming, just the way Alice liked it.

Alice made a ridiculous circle in the snow as she spun to see the tall, slender tree piercing through the forest of pines. The broken branch lay like a ramp for the entertainment of tiny forest animals. "At least the limb isn't in the creek." Alice hiked through the snow, handsaw at the ready.

"Remember to cut them at least as long as my arm so we can trim them at the house." Violet coached.

"Yes, my love. I remember." Alice smiled knowingly at Violet.

Minutes later, the limbs were sectioned into eight pieces that were approximately the length of Violet's arm.

"Backpack, please." Alice looked skyward as large fluffy flakes dropped into the open bag.

With the load of logs hoisted over her shoulder, Alice followed her tracks back to the snow-covered car. "It had to snow, didn't it?" she said aloud to herself. With the bag half hanging off her shoulder, Alice opened the rear cargo space of their car. The lift supports squealed as the hatchback raised.

"Bess needs some grease," Violet joked.

"Bess is just fine as she is," Alice said as the bag of logs thumped onto the rubber mat. She closed the hatch and patted the tail light as she walked around to the driver's side. Their Subaru Outback, better known as Bess, was on the verge of hitting three-hundred-thousand miles, and was eight months older than their relationship. This car was a part of their lives, so they had planned a party to commemorate the turning of the odometer. If Alice's estimates were accurate, that three-hundred-thousand mile mark would occur during their drive to celebrate solstice with Aunt Eunice.

"Are you ready for this trip?" Violet tugged her gloves off and wedged them in the gap between the seats. Her hat was next, releasing a tangle of salt and pepper black curls, wild enough to capture the heart of the woman beside her. Highlights of gray were beginning to show but neither of them really cared about it.

"I'm more excited about rolling Bess's odometer over than I am about Yule this year." Alice reached across the armrest to hold Violet's hand. "Three-hundred-thousand miles is a lifetime." The heat blasting from the dashboard vent made the perfect hand warmer.

"Twenty years. There are so many memories here." Violet smiled as she thought about the Bess 'misunderstanding' instigated by their friend Brittney:

*"Brittney says that some girl named Bess is your first love," Violet said as they sat by the fire waiting for their tin cups of coffee to cool. Technically this wasn't any kind of date since the two of them were spending the next few weeks together hiking through the national forest.*

*"Britt, the bitch." Alice laughed. "She's such a pain in the ass."*

*"So, Bess isn't a girlfriend?" The look of hope in Violet's eyes, and the way the flames of the fire caused the light brown to twinkle, made Alice's heart beat a little faster.*

*"Bess isn't even a friend." Alice chuckled as she poked a stick at the smoldering log. "Bess is my new car and Britt is going to have a hard time hiking out of here after I take her gear and leave her in the woods."*

*"Party of one in the forest?" Violet joked. Her lips formed a perfect tiny 'O' before blowing across the top of her mug.*

*Alice shook her head. "Uh, yeah. Whatever it is, she's not going to like it."*

Violet laughed at the memory as she said. "Party of two in the forest this time."

Alice remembered with a bittersweet smile. "Yeah, two."

"Sorry to revisit—"

Alice interrupted. "No sorries. There were a lot of good times to go with the bad but at least we're all here, mostly, and it's time for a trip." It had been almost a full six weeks since she'd thought about Britt, and those weeks without nightmares often felt like a lifetime. She needed to call her friend and catch up, but she wasn't ready for the dark dreams, the memories that always followed their conversations even after twenty years.

Thinking about the drive to Aunt Eunice's place for the solstice celebration was the mood change she needed. Alice had spent an entire Sunday afternoon planning the three-day route from their two-bedroom house in the Pacific Northwest to Aunt Eunice's cottage in the middle of the Great Basin. They would stop to visit a former hiking-buddy and business partner, Stacey, who was building her roller derby empire. But the most vital stop on the drive was to take that once-in-a-lifetime odometer picture at the national forest.

They had returned to that park a few times while Alice struggled with flashbacks, but not everything about that trip had been tragic. Violet was on the trip to avoid her familial commitments, as most twenty-somethings fresh out of college did. It definitely wasn't love at first sight; in fact, Alice had been so frustrated with Violet's presence she had almost kicked her off the trail.

"Personality conflicts made great love stories," they joked often in the early days of their relationship, and their life together was certainly a testament to that. There was also mutual respect and a heavy dose of surviving a traumatic experience. They saved each other in different ways and that was what endured.

"We've lived an amazing life with Bess." Alice tipped her finger against the faded pride flag dangling from the mirror.

"We have, my love." Vi cocked her body against the armrest on the car door.

Alice took her wife's hand and raised it for a kiss. "Party of two in the forest," she confirmed.

"It's going to be absolutely perfect," Violet said as her head relaxed against the seat.

# CHAPTER TWO

"I don't think that's eighteen inches." Violet stretched the end of the measuring tape alongside the aspen log. The haul from the hike was spread out over the top of the plastic-covered work table in Violet's photography space.

Alice wore her toolbelt half-hitched on her hip. She swiped at the sawdust on her flannel shirt – detritus from trimming each log on the front porch. "Honey, I measured them twice and they're all exactly the size your aunt wants them." She squeezed the trigger on the drill to lock the half-inch paddle bit into the keyless chuck. "You did a great job on the ribbons, too. They're thatched nice and tight." She paused. "I double-checked all the knots."

Violet's head turned abruptly. "You did not check the knots on a Yule log?"

Alice was poking fun and knew that Violet might poke back. "Of course I did. I'm a climber."

"That's so not funny." Violet bumped her hip. "You're never going to let me forget about how terrible I was at knots when we met."

"Terrible is an understatement." Alice threaded her finger beneath the gap in the logs. "My life was going to be in your incapable-of-tying hands." She grinned her toothy smile attempting to say her unpopular phrase.

"Knots save lives." Violet interrupted, before her wife could begin the sentence. "Yes, love, I remember."

"That's because you had a great teacher," Alice said proudly, shining her knuckles on her shirt.

"Yes, Brittney was the absolute best."

The mention of the name made Alice pause. "Oh, ouch."

"Well, she spent hours with me while you were the team leader being all serious and broody," Violet poked.

"It was my job." Alice revved the drill again.

"And you took it very seriously." Violet bumped her again. "And you were broody."

"Yes, I did take it seriously and we all survived, even if – and I say 'if' because by my definition I never was – I was broody."

"Yeah, I'll let you believe that." They fell into the silliness of their shared memory. Alice clapped her hands, snapping back to focus on the unfinished project. "The logs are tied tightly." She held Violet's hand. "Well done."

"Thank you." Violet patted her wife's hip.

"You're welcome."

Violet opened the bottle on the table and poured the liquid across the aspen bundle, drenching the logs in the Yule-oil concoction.

Alice waved her hand to disperse the strength of the aromatic blend. She read from the list of ingredients written in Aunt Eunice's scrolling penmanship. "Mugwort is for?"

"Protection," Violet shared. "It also amps-up the energies drawn from the earth during the celebration."

"I remember the earth energy part. I feel that surge when Eunice lights the log."

"It's pretty powerful." Violet plucked at a curl of bark. "Like the cedar and cinnamon used to boost positivity in Auntie's home."

"That's definitely a positive space to be in any time of the year."

"It is."

Alice picked up the ingredient list. "I know why we used juniper berries."

Violet smiled. "Your favorite is easy to remember because you smeared it all over my leg."

"You were bitten by a snake." Alice grinned.

Violet shook her head. "It was never a snake and you know it."

"How else was I going to explain my hands on your legs?"

"Juniper berries and snakes seemed completely plausible."

"I panicked."

"It was adorable." Violet said.

"Adorable wasn't what I was shooting for at the time."

"I remember what you were shooting for." Violet hip-bumped her wife playfully.

"I got the girl in the end." Alice sniffed the empty bottle before replacing the cap."Aunt Eunice's no-longer-secret recipe is such a sense memory."

"It is," Violet affirmed. "For so many reasons it'll always make me think of family."

"It will." Alice revved the drill before placing the bit on the log bundle. "After I drill these holes we can add pinecones and the rest of the mistletoe cuttings."

Violet stretched on her toes to kiss her wife. "Perfect, but that log looks longer than the rest." She patted the piece ends again with her palm. Although the scent of Yule was in the air, it wouldn't be complete without her aunt Eunice's hard-working hands to light the enchanting flames. The tradition of starting the log by sacred candlelight was Aunt Eunice's personal touch.

Alice pulled the measuring tape out. "Nope, they're right. Again!" The flexible tape rolled back into the case and she tucked it into the tool belt. "The limbs are cut. That part is done and perfect." The drill revved and Alice bored three holes to anchor the candles into the aspen bundle. They'd followed Eunice's plan for preparation with precision. She revved the drill twice to reverse the bit loose and put the tools in their case. "My job is done here. All of the pretty frilly bits are in your gorgeous hands. Work your magic." She jiggled her fingers imitating magic hands waving over the logs. "Tie and glue those ribbons, woman."

Violet delivered a broom and dustpan, picking up all of the bits left behind from the drill. "One more job."

"Right, clean up my mess." Alice poured the scraps into the tinder bucket beside the fireplace.

Violet lowered the temperature on the warming pot to keep the pine pitch in liquid form, and the aroma filled the room. She wrapped and tied the eight individual aspen cuttings, looping them together to become one festive bundle. Yule logs weren't meant to be complicated but every part needed to disappear into the flames without leaving unnatural waste.

"This looks pretty good," Violet said as she tucked the cut end of the mistletoe into the warm pine pitch she used as glue.

"I like that in our world, mistletoe isn't for non-consensual kisses," Alice said.

"It's for love, and only consensual," Violet added.

"We've totally got this." Alice raised her hand for a high five and Violet slapped hers against it.

"We absolutely killed it." Vi glued the knots on the red cording and held the candles up to check for size. "The holes are perfect. I'm going to wait to set the candles so we can fit the Yule log into the plastic tote." She wrapped the ten-inch tapers in linen and placed them in the bottom of the container. "This sweet project gets to take a little ride in Bess."

"I'm glad we picked up the fifty-quart bin because my eighteen inch cuts…" She paused when Violet playfully nudged her shoulder. "Ouch."

Vi waved the container lid, creating a fan effect to cool her wife. "I get it. You cut them to the perfect size."

"Exactly, that makes me right again." She licked her fingertip and stroked a line in the air. The storage container had narrow gaps on the end leaving space for their Yule creation to fit tight and safe for their eleven-hundred mile journey.

Before locking the lid in place, Violet drizzled what was left of their Yule oil over the top of everything. "Practically perfect."

"Just like my wife." Alice dropped her arm around Violet's shoulder.

"And just like mine."

~~~~~~~~~~

The suitcase popped one step at a time as Violet dragged it from the front door. Alice was double-checking Bess's tire pressure for the third time. The tires were new, added just in time for the drive, and Alice was excited to put these particular trip-miles on them. She tucked the pressure gauge into the tool kit stowed with the spare tire, confirming again that Bess was road-trip ready.
~~~~~~~~~~

Violet, unfortunately, was not. "I put a raincoat in the suitcase. It might be dumb for this time of year." She kicked at the carry-on sized hard-shelled case covered in stickers from the destinations they'd traveled to over their twenty-year relationship. It was definitely more than she needed for the week.

"Be prepared and all that." Alice held out her hand to take the suitcase.

Violet turned around again, the case handle gripped tight. "I should take walking shoes, or hiking boots." She turned around for a third time, making Alice dizzy from the circles.

"We aren't going to hike, love. Car ride, picnic at the park, car ride." Alice ticked the items off on her fingers.

"What about cameras?"

"Use your phone on this trip. You can get fancy with that and it's one less..."

"But they're my cameras."

"The only big photo moment we have planned is for Bess's odometer. Your phone will be easiest. Trust me and keep it light."

"Right, pack light and anything we might need we can pick up along the way." She rolled the bag towards her wife.

"So, you're ready to hit the road?" Alice wedged her duffle bag between the Yule log tote and Violet's rolling carry-on suitcase.

"The audiobook finished downloading and I'm ready. I think." Alice opened the door for her. Before Violet sat down, she held up her phone to show the image of an abandoned house on the screen. "You're going to love this one, I promise."

"It looks Samhain spooky, not very winter-holiday festive." Alice leaned in the open door.

"It is spooky and who says we have to wait for Samhain to enjoy ghosts and scary stories?"

"Obviously not you." Alice closed her wife's door, making a final circle around the car before getting in the driver's seat. She took a moment to enjoy her position and appreciate Bess. The dashboard of the Outback was original, vintage, even, for some, and as unchanged as the day Alice picked her out.

She smiled at Violet who was with her almost as long as she'd had Bess. They'd fallen in love in this car, dreamed their life dreams together in it and Alice was excited to celebrate the three-hundred-thousand mile landmark. "Pop that adapter cord in." She pointed to the cassette dangling from the radio as she tugged the seatbelt over her shoulder.

"You know, we could upgrade to a wireless hi-tech stereo," Violet suggested. This conversation came up almost every time they loaded Bess for a long drive.

Alice's gasp was ridiculously exaggerated as she clutched her non-existent pearls to her chest. The ring of keys dangled from her finger, the river stone tapping against her breast. There was history in that shiny red rock and it had everything to do with their future picnic location. That red rock was more than a symbol of their love. "Honey, you can't abruptly change someone like that. You're going to hurt Bess's feelings."

Violet raised her eyebrow. "I swear, if she could come inside the house I might actually be jealous of your first love." She laughed as she plugged the adapter cord into the bottom of her phone.

Alice rubbed her hand across the dashboard. "Oh Bess, cover your car ears, baby. Don't listen to big old mean Violet Hadley-Crest. She doesn't know what she's talking about. I can love you right here in the garage." She kissed her fingertips and touched them to the steering wheel.

"Did you just call me old?" Violet turned in her seat as she locked the seatbelt over her chest.

"Yep, big and mean, too." She left the key dangling from the ignition. "We've got a long drive ahead so I'm making sure Bess is rolling out the door as happy as possible."

"And what about Violet rolling out happy?"

Alice laughed. "It's three miles to the gas station. You get three miles to be mad at me and then we're going to drive happily."

"You know exactly how I work." Violet crossed her arms. She remembered the day she'd met her wife: the nervous introduction, the misspoken comment about 'Al' actually being Alice and her realization that her guide was not the man she'd expected to lead her hiking excursion. It was the beginning of their push and pull relationship and Violet's inability to reconcile her attraction to a woman who was far from her previous, feminine type.

Growing up in a 'family values' filled home left Violet isolated and alone in her struggle with identity and sexuality. Alice broke the mold and also didn't waste precious time on self-defeating feelings. Three miles was a long distance to linger in an emotional state on a hike, but they weren't hiking today.

"That's less than five minutes to be mad at you for reducing me to big, old and mean."

"Since you are mostly none of those, in the flesh, I think you can manage." Alice turned the key in the ignition. "Get out the map." She pointed to the glovebox. "Please."

"You realize," Violet said as the door on the dashboard dropped open, "a new radio would have a GPS?"

"Three miles." Alice turned the car onto the street and stopped at the first light. "Bess is just fine and what else would you have to do if you weren't navigating?"

Violet opened the auto club's spiral-bound booklet. "I get it. This is the way we go to Auntie's house."

"This is how we get it done. Let's not break our twenty-year record." Alice hesitated before reaching across the armrest. "Do you need all three miles?"

Violet looked at her. "Yep, I would appreciate all three."

Minutes later, they pulled into the gas station. Violet clipped the map to the band on the dashboard before her wife opened her door.

"You are neither big nor old." Alice turned her hand over on the gear shift, offering an affirming touch.

"Thank you." Violet wasn't about to mention the mean part because she knew in her heart she had a bitterness that most people couldn't overlook. Her wife's ability to overlook it was one of the things she found most charming about her. There was simple perfection in the way they loved.

Al pointed with her eyes toward the dash of the car.

"You're a magical car, Bess." Violet patted and rubbed the dash.

"Perfect." Alice leaned over to kiss her wife. "Just. Like. You."

# CHAPTER THREE

Alice tapped the pause button on the phone mounted to the dashboard. The audiobook plot was at the part where most people with common sense would run away from the obvious danger. The two main characters did not, and Alice was frustrated. "I can't believe she's going into that building." She gestured at the phone screen. "They heard the child's whisper. And there's no one there. There was no child in physical form." She was steering with her knee as she tugged the longer length of her hair into a messy top-of-the-head bun. "This book is creepy. Why is she going in there?"

Violet, ever the cheerleader, said, "It's their job. I think it's kinda brave, don't you?"

Alice snickered. "Maybe, but mostly reckless. Her partner, he's dopey for following her inside that building. He said he heard noises that might be voices too. That's a clear sign to get the hell outta there, not to go inside."

"You say that," Violet turned with her back resting against the door, "but you'd be the first one in there to investigate."

Alice reached to press play. "Maybe I would, but it would still be brave with a side order of recklessness."

~~~~~~~~~~

Violet pushed pause on the audiobook before reaching toward the back seat. "Trail mix or jerky?" She held up the
~~~~~~~~~~

resealable bag containing their trip snacks, oblivious to the abrupt interruption of the story.

"How could you stop it there?" Alice squealed.

The main character was running to find her partner, who wasn't answering the phone. The building was occupied by a non-human entity and the investigation had taken a sinister turn. It was definitely a climactic moment.

Alice's mouth was wide open, her head tilted as she waited for an answer to her question.

"I need a snack." Violet shrugged. "Trail mix or Jerky?"

"Gummy bears dipped in chocolate?" Alice asked.

"Those are for the celebration when we stop for pictures," Violet explained. "Right now you can have nuts and berries or the flesh of a wild beast."

"Wild beast?" Alice raised her eyebrow. "Gosh, I love you."

"I know." Violet held up the packaged meat. "So yeah, wild beast is actually turkey jerky from Jackson's nephew's treacherous backyard."

"Sounds exactly right. I'll take the wild beast and maybe more water from the canteen." Alice leaned over with kissy fish lips and her wife planted a kiss on them.

"Press play," Alice begged.

Violet mumbled, "Yes, dear," as she shoved a strip of turkey jerky into her wife's mouth.

~~~~~~~~~~

"This says seventeen miles." Violet flipped the page of the map back and forth after pausing the audiobook again. "What does the odometer read?" she asked as she stretched over the center to lean in for a look.
~~~~~~~~~~

"Two-hundred and ninety-nine thousand, nine-hundred and eighty-one. We're nineteen miles from our goal." She tucked her fingers into the lowest part of the steering wheel after signaling to exit the interstate highway.

"So we make a lap around the park." Violet's smile was big, her dimples deep, creating tiny lines in the corners of her eyes. Alice called them her joy wrinkles and it was a pure expression of happiness without any hang ups on patriarchal beauty standards.

"As many laps as we need to hit the mark." Alice reached between her wife's knees, dipping into the snack bag. "Apple?"

"I'll wait until we have our picnic in the park."

Alice took a big bite, crunching loud as she chewed. The apple was small, and she was almost to the seeds in five bites. She dropped the core into the garbage bag dangling off the shift handle.

Violet pulled a hand wipe from the pouch in the door and passed it to her wife. At the same time, she noticed a change in mood. "What's going on in that head of yours, my love?"

Alice smiled and finished chewing as she wiped her hand. "I was thinking about you, and how we got here." She tipped her head toward the view out the window.

"It's been a ride, hasn't it, my love?" She opened her palm to take the nearly-dry wipe.

Alice gripped Violet's hand instead. "I fell in love with you here."

Vi laughed. "You hated me here, at first."

Alice squeezed her fingers around Violet's hand. "I didn't hate you. I just didn't like you very much."

"Yeah, we've come a very long way." Violet stretched to look at the odometer as they pulled up to the park entrance. "We're so close." She was almost giddy.

Alice rolled down the window as they approached the park kiosk to pay the park ranger for a day pass, her eyes still on Violet. As she turned toward the window she looked up at a familiar face smiling widely back at her.

"Holy shit, Al-fucking-Hadley!" The ranger tipped her hat back to uncover her face.

"Britt, my Bitch! No damn way you're here!" Alice shifted the car into park and jumped out of the vehicle. The hug was tight and long and neither wanted to let the other go. The ranger's feet left the ground before Alice set her down.

"What the hell are you doing here?" Britt leaned in closer to look into the car. "Violet, girl, how's it going?"

"It's going ten times better now that I'm seeing you." Violet leaned across the car. "What the hell are you doing back in the park?"

"Long short story—" Britt looked up to see a car pulling in behind them. She made change for Alice, passed her the day-pass ticket and said, "Circle behind the shack and park by my truck. I'll be right there."

Alice drove around the corner and pulled into grass and gravel patch parking directly beside the pickup truck stamped with the national park logo. She turned the car off and thought about the ins-and-outs of the hiking trails in the park. Britt, also known as Brittney Phelps, was one of Alice's favorite people, an experienced guide and although they didn't share a romantic history, they did share a powerful and nearly tragic past. "How cool is it that Britt is back in this park? Did you know?"

Violet paused to consider the question, thinking about the national park and the history the three of them shared. "She's back in the park, and no, I didn't know, but I think it's pretty amazing."

"How perfect is it that she's here? And today of all days. She's the one who drooled over Bess's color." Alice was practically bouncing in her seat. "The way she flipped through that brochure. Sounded like someone hooking up in a magazine, but we drove Bess together on that first day."

"I remember the stories." Violet smiled. "Red makes it go faster." She repeated the twenty-year-old joke that was meant to sway Alice's decision to purchase Bess.

Before either could complete the punchline, a park-ranger-ball-capped head popped through the open driver-side window so Britt could add, "And chicks dig red." She laughed as she tapped the roof of the car. "I can't believe Bess is still on the road." She opened the rear door and sat inside, scooting to the middle. "Hiya, Bess." Britt rubbed the center console with her three-fingered hand and patted the seat.

"I can't believe the two of you and this car." Violet shook her head, the disgust a complete ruse because she loved Bess, too.

Britt smiled. "We had plans to meet so many sporty hot chicks in this car."

"I've heard *those* stories too." Violet turned in her seat. "You're looking so good, Britt."

"Feeling pretty good, too." Britt scooted to wedge against the middle of the console. "What brings you home?"

"Home," Alice whispered. In a sense this *was* one of many homes she cherished before settling into life with her wife.

"Celebrating a milestone," Violet said.

"Oh yeah?" Britt asked, taking a quick peek at the ranger booth. "You knocked her up?" She laughed at her own joke.

"Absolutely not!" they said at the same time.

"So, what is it?"

Vi answered. "Bess is about a half mile from three hundred thousand."

"No shit?" Britt pulled on the driver's seat-back to squeeze in for a look at the odometer. Alice keyed the ignition to activate the display. "No shit."

Alice reached over her shoulder, touching Britt's three-fingered hand. She raised her eyes to the rearview mirror, and shared a knowing glance with Britt. "I'm happy you're back in the park," she said, before her hand fell away.

"They say you gotta get back on the horse and that's what I needed to do."

"It looks good on you." Violet smiled.

"Thanks." Britt relaxed against the seat of the car. "So, you're celebrating?"

"I think we're going to have a picnic wherever we hit the three-hundred-thousand mileage mark," Alice said.

"Still the romantic," Britt teased.

"Always and forever." Violet smiled as she felt strong fingers squeeze her own.

"You got any gummy bears for the celebration?" Britt fished around in the cooler bag.

"Chocolate covered," Violet said. "In that container."

Britt was already unscrewing the cap. "You never let me down."

"Those are all Violet, this time," Alice said.

The park ranger's face popped forward to plant a kiss on Violet's cheek. "Thanks, beautiful." A car horn interrupted their conversation and Britt reached for the handle of the door. "Gotta go, lovebirds. Keep safe and protect yourselves." She took the container of candy with her.

"Roger that and we'll check in with you before we take off." Alice started the car.

"Violet, make sure you keep her in line. It was good to see you, Al."

"Al." Violet whispered the name, but Alice and Britt heard the shortened version spoken in a melancholy tone.

Twenty years ago, Alice despised the long version of her name, which was a grating reminder of the girl who was never enough for her family. The first time they'd met, that conflict was the first battle between the would-be lovers, a fierce test of wills, and like so many arguments over their twenty years, Violet had a great offense to Alice's defensive walls. It had been so long since Alice scolded Violet for calling her by her given name. Twenty years ago, everyone called her Al. Everyone but Violet.

Violet laughed at Britt's suggestion that anyone could keep Alice from a decision made. "After twenty years, I'm not even going to try to keep her in line. Not a chance."

"Then at the very least, keep her on the trails." Britt banged her knuckles on the roof of the car.

"You can count on that." Violet blew her a kiss. "We'll see you on the way out." She turned in her seat, waiting for Alice to digest their interaction. After so many years together, she knew where her wife's thoughts would land.

"She looks good," Alice whispered, her voice breaking on the last word.

"Mh-hmm," Violet agreed.

"The limp's mostly gone."

"It's been twenty years, love." Violet rubbed the back of her wife's hand.

"The inside scars are the hardest." Alice's eyes skimmed to the rearview mirror and she watched her friend speak animatedly to the patron at the ranger booth. She remembered all of their scars.

"Maybe her nightmares are like yours?" Violet asked.

Al shook her head as she looked at her wife. "Maybe." She didn't say another word as she shifted Bess into gear and pulled out onto the park roadway. "Less than a mile. I think we'll stop at the first trailhead and celebrate."

"We're changing the subject, now?" Violet opened the glove box, intentionally avoiding eye contact with her wife.

"We're putting a pin in this subject because today is supposed to be about celebrating, and I know the next eight hundred miles will include a conversation about moving on and PTSD resources." She said the entire sentence in one breath. "Plus, we're here and the odometer hasn't turned."

Violet tucked the map inside the folder in the glove box and leaned over to look at the gauge. "Huh."

"Huh," Alice repeated, with a hint of sarcasm. "That's all you got?"

"Well, maybe you should back up." Violet waved her hand as if she could guide the vehicle with the motion.

"Back up and go forward until we hit three hundred thousand?" Alice chuckled as she smiled. "That seems like cheating, or somehow violating a rule."

"There are rules for turning the dial thingies on an odometer?" Violet looked over her shoulder. "Just back up the length of this road and I'll bet we hit it."

They did not hit it; in fact, they made three fifty-yard passes before the dial on the odometer turned toward their goal. Alice had tears in her eyes and Violet pulled out a tiny New Years Eve horn and a party popper from beneath her seat. The bang made Alice jump and the tiny pieces of streamer and confetti flew everywhere.

"We made it to three hundred thousand. I can't believe it." Alice palmed the steering wheel, blasting the horn in celebration. "We have to take a picture." She transformed into the secretly playful woman Violet had fallen in love with. "I was thinking I could stick my face down in the dash and you could—"

Violet interrupted. "I've got a better idea." She hopped out of the car, ran around and opened Alice's door. "Come with me." She tugged her wife's wrist and, as she exited, tiny bits of confetti fell to the ground.

"You're going to pick that up." Alice pointed to the specks of paper.

"Completely biodegradable and made from plants, which are natural materials." Violet blew her a kiss. "Paid out the ass for them, but I knew it was the first thing you'd worry about." She kissed Alice. "Happy wife, happy life."

Before Alice could reply, she felt her body being tugged to the front of the car.

"Lay on the hood."

"What?" Alice's eyebrows scrunched as she shook her head. "I'm not climbing on Bess like some cheesy car show chick."

"Ooh, nice thought." Violet pictured her hard-core woman stretched across the hood of the car and found the image delicious.

"Stop it. We are not getting kicked out of this park because you can't keep your pants on."

"I wasn't thinking about my pants." Vi winked as her eyes raked over Alice's body.

"Woman!"

Violet shook away the thoughts. "Okay, back to plan A. Lay half over the hood, on those gorgeous abs, and stare through the windshield."

"I'm going to dent her hood." Alice was too practical about the entire scenario.

"You will not. She's a tough girl and can handle your burl." The wink was playful, with full dimples, and Violet knew her wife would cave.

Alice was cautious as she leveled one leg on the hood, leaving the other on the ground. Her nearly six-foot height and long legs made the position effortless. "How about one foot on and one foot off?"

"Oh, it's like that night right before our first kiss. We weren't even in bed but somehow you thought having a foot on the ground would keep it virtuous." Violet's tongue tipped out of her lips as she joked.

"Baby, you know you wanted me, and twenty years later you still want me." Alice teased Violet through the windshield's glass.

"I believe I thought you were hot, that's all." Violet tilted the steering wheel, adjusting so the angle would include the dashboard display of the odometer. She pressed the brake, keyed the ignition and the numbers displayed. "Hold on. I'm moving forward a little." She pulled the car up a few feet to get a perfect angle with sunlight across her wife's face.

"More warning next time." Alice's fingers clenched the hood at the base of the windshield. "Always the photographer."

"Darn right. Now smile." Violet held the phone, attempting to adjust the dashboard and Alice's wide smile into the frame. "You have to get closer to the windshield."

Alice shoved her body forward. "Better?"

"Yes, the light is perfect." Violet smiled as the phone's camera focused on the car's odometer with Alice framed in the background. She took a rapid succession of photos, pausing to scroll through. Her hands shook with excitement. "I can't believe how perfect this is." She held her phone to the glass.

"I can't see with the reflection," Alice yelled.

Without hesitation, Violet jumped out to share the series of pictures. "Look." The car was running and in gear as she exited the car. "Oh shit!"

Alice's eyes went wide as the car rolled with her half on top. "Vi, hit the brake." Her foot dragged across the gravel as the car continued forward. The open door hit Violet in the back, slamming closed and knocking her to the ground. It was a perfectly imperfect storm in slow motion as Bess gained momentum in the direction of the steering wheel's position, away from Violet, tossing Alice to the ground. The small dip in the parking lot's pitch encouraged the motion of an untethered vehicle as they watched Bess roll directly into the tree. The impact echoed around them.

Alice scrambled to her feet. "I can't believe it," she said as she stared at the impact point. "What just happened?"

"Are you alright?" Violet asked as she stepped toward the car. The glass from the headlight crunched beneath her feet as she looked around to see the impact point of the tree limb.

"Oh, Vi." Alice's hands fell limp to her side. "How?"

“Baby, I was just excited about the pictures.”

Alice opened the car door. “Bess.” She sat staring at the oak leaf branch poking through the windshield. Her eyes locked on the three-hundred-thousand mile indicator. “Oh, Bess.”

# CHAPTER FOUR

The amber and white bar glowing on top of Britt's park ranger vehicle zigged back and forth as the tow truck beeped its reverse warning alarm. It would have felt like a festival of lights if the flashing colors weren't an indication of Bess's accident.

The car's hood was covered with acorn caps, scattered nut shells and knobby debris from the fallen limbs. Leaves flopped, practically defying science where they'd wedged beneath the wiper blades. The combination of the single crushed headlight and the leaves made Bess look like one of the horror victims from their audiobook. Everything, including the windshield damage, made the red Subaru Outback completely unsafe to drive.

"It doesn't look *too* bad," Violet said, doing her best to be optimistic as she lifted the Yule tote from the trunk of the car. The plastic debris from the side mirror was almost pretty as it caught the light's reflection, but Vi didn't dare mention this observation.

"It's not *bad*, bad, but her hood," Alice whimpered as she picked a sliver of bark from a crack in the metal, "and her door." She winced when her boots crunched on the broken reflective material, eliminating the light dance Vi was quietly admiring. "And her windshield." The sorrow in her voice was so much like a child who had just fallen off her bike while licking an ice cream cone.

"All this stuff is fixable," the tow-truck driver interrupted. "This is low impact," he said, pointing to the hood, "and mostly cosmetic."

He reached for the keys in Alice's hands but she pulled them away. The red stone dangling on the ring clunked her knuckles. The rock wrapped in copper wire was more than an ornament and she wouldn't leave it behind. She tried to put it in her pocket but it slipped from her hand, landing in the remains of the driver's side mirror.

"Bess is my baby." Alice picked up the stone and a piece of fractured mirror, staring in to see her reflection. "We're supposed to take pictures where we fell in love, and we spent two days making that for Aunt Eunice." She pointed at the perfectly-intact Yule log container. "There's no way we can drive Bess now."

Violet slipped loose strands of silver-brown hair over her ear. She saw the tears in Alice's eyes. "The tow truck guy says—" She leaned to look at the name patch stitched to the man's shirt. "Pete. Pete says Bess can be fixed."

"But there's no way to drive her today?" The hope in Alice's eyes faded as Pete shook his head in response to the question.

"Sorry, your girl Bess is gonna need parts. She's more than five years old so we don't keep them in stock at the garage. Two days at best for everything," he said. "Three if I need to replace the hood."

The way that Pete referred to Bess was more than kind, boosting Alice's confidence in his abilities to service the twenty-year-old vehicle.

"We can rent a car," Violet offered.

Alice's pout under normal circumstances was adorable but her defeated expression, along with her hand caressing Bess's trunk, was heartbreaking. "It's not the same if we rent a car."

"I know, love." Violet stacked the bags on top of the Yule log tote, her small suitcase upright beside it. Alice watched, mostly glaring as the team in charge of tree services cut the limbs to haul them away.

"Call this guy," Britt said as she held up her phone. The website, with a smiley-face emoji logo for the shop, displayed on the screen.

"Happy Car Rental?" Alice frowned. "You're kidding, right?"

"Don't judge. They're great and with a last-minute rental, he'll treat you right."

Alice was skeptical as she typed the information into her phone to do her own search for reviews and ratings. It was a mixed list, averaging three and a half stars, but what choice did they really have?

Britt tapped the number on her own phone and called. "Ricky!" Her enthusiasm was intense and echoed through the parking lot. It was obvious Britt and Ricky had a history. "My guy. I have an emergency rental for you and they're my very best friends." She winked at Violet as she paused to listen. "I know, man. Hit me with what you've got." Seconds later, she pulled the phone from her ear to see an image in the text message she'd received. She studied the picture of a compact-sized car and put the phone back to her ear. "That's the only rental you have?"

Alice leaned closer, trying to get a look at the image before it disappeared. "This doesn't sound promising," she whispered to her wife.

Violet forced a smile. "We don't have much of a choice. We're kinda stuck here if we don't find something."

Alice tapped the plastic Yule log tote with the tip of her boot. "And we thought the knee-deep snowstorm to get the Aspen log was the glitch."

"It'll be fun, just—"

Britt interrupted. "I gave Ricky your name and number."

"Okay." Alice's attention was on the tow-truck driver who was attaching chains and hooks to Bess. She knew a slow roll back and upward onto the flatbed trailer was coming. Without looking away, she asked, "What does he have for us?"

"It's compact." Britt's voice hitched, obviously unhappy and unable to hide her hesitation.

"How compact?" Alice asked, her forehead screwing up in response to the squeal of the flatbed trailer tilting. Bess was going to be fine. She chanted in her head as the hydraulics hissed and vibrated during the slow leveling procedure.

"Um." Britt hesitated, which irritated Alice.

"How compact, Britt?"

"Fiat 500 compact."

Alice thought about the car, running through her limited memory of Fiat's line of vehicles. "That's a damn clown car." She held her hand up, pinching her fingers, making a gap an inch apart. "It's, like, this big."

"Come on, Al, it's the only car he's got so close to the holidays," Britt explained. "I'd give you my truck but the forest service owns it." She pointed to the vehicle behind them, the light bar still flashing back and forth to warn of the accident scene.

"Nice call, and you're right," Violet said. "We can make it work as long as this fits in the back." She tapped her toe to their celebratory Yule log beside the duffle bag of Alice's clothing, Violet's small suitcase, and their collapsible picnic cooler.

"It'll fit," Pete said as he scribbled numbers from Alice's road service card onto the service form fastened to his grease-smudged aluminum clipboard. "They sure are like clown cars. In fact, I think Ricky makes one up for the pride parade every year."

"Really?" Violet and Alice questioned. Ricky sounded like a quirky character.

"Oh yeah, he's the noisiest bell at the ball." Pete pulled the handle on the flatbed to lock the leveled car into position. "If you want, I can give you a ride to Ricky's rental place."

"That'd be great," Violet said. She watched her wife examining the chains and tie-downs holding Bess to the flatbed.

"You've got her on there well?" Alice asked, critical of the situation. Her anxiety was obvious by the tight shoulders and clenched fists.

"Perfectly fit as can be." Pete flipped a few handles and turned a knob on the control panel. "Trust me, this isn't my first rodeo."

"Great." Alice's tone lacked confidence.

Britt tugged Alice's shoulder. "Keep in touch with me over the next few days," she whispered. "I'll take care of Bess until you come back." Britt's tone, and the way she knew how to direct Alice, was the calm they all needed in this storm.

Violet couldn't help but remember how the ranger's quick reaction, her complete lack of concern for her personal safety, was the greatest reason they were all alive.

Britt threw an arm around Alice's shoulder and slow-walked her friend to the cab of the tow truck. With a bouncing stretch, Alice and Violet were up inside, their laps holding bags and a bin with the ornate Yule log inside. Pete pumped the brakes on his truck, honked his horn at Britt and started the eight-mile drive to the rental car facility.

It was not the storefront Violet expected as they pulled up. The canopy had streamers of garland twinkling in multiple colors, welcoming travelers for the holidays. The front window had a glittery pride flag, a menorah and, overhead, a string of gold moons and stars. In the middle of nowhere, Ricky was absolutely an inclusive guy.

"My station is two blocks away," Pete said, as he pulled up to Happy Car Rental. "I can drop you here or you can wander over from the garage when we're done." The red Fiat 500 was parked in front and a smiley-faced person stood at the gas pump filling the car with fuel.

"Red makes it go faster?" Violet pointed at the tiny car, hopeful her wife would laugh, but Alice was not amused.

"We're going to drive sixteen-hundred miles in that?" Alice's head slumped against the passenger window of the tow truck as the vehicle lurched to a stop.

"It's that or the wrath of Aunt Eunice," Violet laughed nervously.

Alice patted the tote wedged between her knees, consuming all of her space. "Your aunt will never trust us to deliver again if we don't arrive on schedule."

"Clown car it is." Violet kissed her wife. "I'll go in and rent. You go with Pete to get Bess settled." Divide and conquer was the decision, and by the time Alice returned to the rental car location, Violet had wedged all of the bags into the tiniest of back seats and trunk.

"This is the most ridiculous car I've ever seen. Who needs a car this small?" Alice pushed the lever to adjust the driver's seat position.

"I thought you were the adventurous one?" Violet turned in her seat as she tugged the belt across her shoulder.

"Can you imagine for a minute how much razzing we're going to get when we roll up to Auntie's house in this?" She adjusted the steering wheel, noticing the odometer reading. "It's got ninety-thousand miles on it." She scrunched her brow as she shook her head. "Have you ever rented a car with that many miles on it?"

"Honey, I've never rented a car." Violet opened her window to release the overpowering aroma coming from the two air fresheners hanging on the hooks near the rear seats.

"This can't be happening." Alice rolled her window down, letting the unseasonably warm weather move through the interior. She shifted the car into reverse. "Get out the map. Please."

Violet opened the folder she'd removed from Bess and held up the spiral-bound guide created especially for the trip. "Maybe you should let me drive. You seem a little frustrated."

Alice shifted into gear and merged onto the road. "Bess is my baby and I left her with Pete the tow truck guy, in the middle of nowhere. I get to have three miles."

The silence that followed was a sign that all three miles were necessary for Alice to settle her mood. She might need six, but that broke the rules, and they weren't going to add rule breaking to this already-bumpy trip.

Alice's body tensed as she felt the seat back release with a loud click. It reclined, stopped from laying flat by the Yule log tote behind her.

"You alright?" Violet asked as she eyed the route marker on the highway.

"I'm driving a red clown car through nowhere-land on my way to celebrate Yule with a seventy-year-old witch who would probably smack me for disrespecting the pile of logs in the trunk of this thing." Alice reached to readjust the seat, locking and unlocking it back into the uncomfortable reclining position. She was fighting with the clown car and she was not amused.

"But it has turbo." Violet tapped the label on the dashboard.

Alice shook her head and clenched her hands on the steering wheel as she wriggled into a safer driving position.

"So… turbo won't improve the situation?"

"Violet," Alice let out a breath through puffed cheeks. "Bess is smashed."

"I understand that, but it's just a windshield, some lights and a mirror."

"And the bumper and the hood and who knows what—"

Violet interrupted. "It could have been me or you."

Alice blinked slowly and took a breath, almost too long for her position in the driver's seat.

"What if I'd hurt you?" Violet asked. "Bess can be fixed but I don't ever want to do a bloody emergency room again."

Alice's foot slid from the accelerator as she coasted to the stop sign. "It's been twenty years since that bloody ER, but you're right. I don't ever want to do that again either."

They rode in silence for a few miles, listening to the highway noise whip through the poorly-sealed windows. Violet didn't like the front seat, or the adjustments made to accommodate the luggage and tote in the back, but she wasn't going to share any of her discomfort. There was something more important to talk about.

"Britt looked really good," Vi said, forcing the conversation they'd put on hold before the incident.

"I'm not ready to talk about Britt yet." Alice pushed the radio on and the sound of static made the two of them jump. "Sorry." She saw her wife swipe at her cheek and pulled off the road into a sightseeing stop. "Love?"

"I'm sorry, too," Violet said. "I wasn't thinking."

"It's okay." Alice turned her palm up and laid it on her wife's thigh. Violet rubbed their hands, palm to palm. "Bess will be okay and we've officially had our mishap for the trip."

Violet snickered, only half believing they'd be comfortable driving in this machine. "Maybe we can ride along and chill."

"Ride and chill in the clown car," Alice agreed as she chuckled. "Why don't you see if you can connect our audiobook to this thing?"

Violet played with the Bluetooth setting on the phone, and the modes for the audio on the car stereo, to connect the new technology for their drive. She contemplated the paper map over the voiceover directions coming from the GPS, and opted for their original paper plans.

The narration of their murder-mystery audiobook piped through the speakers, and Alice's shoulders relaxed against the driver's seat. "Maybe this won't totally suck after all."

# CHAPTER FIVE

"Three minutes." Alice rested her arms on the steering wheel as she watched the cloud of steam rise from the vents of the car's hood. It was the fourth time on the trip that they'd used the long-established relationship rule of three miles or three minutes to break from whatever tension held them. Right now, it was the Fiat 500 and the mechanical malfunction happening before them.

"Red apparently does not make it go—"

Alice interrupted, pinching her fingers tight on the bridge of her nose. She tried to keep her frustration inside as she whispered, through clenched teeth, "That's all you have to say right now as the two of us are stuck with this." She pointed at the trail of smoke coming from the vents in the hood.

"Maybe it ran out of gas?" Violet offered, having absolutely no experience with cars or the engineering that made them work. This was definitely where their personalities divided.

Alice turned the key again. The grinding and clicking put a frown on her face. They were parked in a scenic view pullout, safe from traffic on the highway, with eighteen new selfies on Violet's phone. The whimsical nature of the smaller woman, and her need to capture their lives in photographs, was Alice's weakness, but all she could think was that they shouldn't have stopped there. "I need three, honey, and there's no way it's out of gas since the gauge reads over half full and this thing runs mostly because hungry gerbils are chasing baby carrots."

Violet snorted. "Why would a car only go woo woo when you turn the key?"

Alice thumped her forehead on the steering wheel. "Woo woo?" She rolled her head to the side to question her wife's observations. "Really, Vi?"

"You're the car person in this family. I'm supposed to tell you when to stop, go, turn left and turn right. I'm the navigator." Violet patted her fingers against the map page.

"Yes and in twenty years have you ever heard me refer to a mechanical problem as a *woo woo*?" She really needed to insist on taking her three minutes.

"Technically no, but we've only had Bess and she's—" Violet caught herself.

"She's not woo woo-ing. She's getting a facelift."

Violet turned her entire body so she could look at her wife. "She's going to be amazing and the bonus is we get to visit Britt on the way home."

"So, bonus Britt is going to make me feel better in this scenario?" Alice waved her hands over the steering wheel as if a magical car fairy would resurrect the dead engine.

"Britt would probably get a kick out of it."

Alice thought for a moment. "Yeah, she definitely would. We probably pushed my old wreck a thousand times before owning Bess."

Violet shifted a shoulder to remove the phone from her pocket. "I'll call the motor club again. You go put the hood up."

"What are the chances we can find another rental car in the middle of the holiday rush?" Alice slapped the key on the dash.

"Another rental car, better than this one?" Vi winked, her dimples deep with a toothy grin.

"You realize I didn't get my three minutes… and you flashed that smile?" She felt around inside the driver's compartment for the engine's hood release. "That's not fair."

"Uh huh." Violet didn't look up from her focus on her phone. "Take your three minutes outside. You can check whatever is happening to the engine while I find us a ride out of here."

Alice laughed and the screen glow lighting her wife's smile was the perfect supplement to the three minute break to soothe her frustration. She raised the hood of the car and wasn't surprised to see the overspray of oil speckling the fiber paper under the hood.

Violet peeked her head around the raised hood, offering a towelette to her wife. "Did the gerbils die?"

"Yep, every last one bit the dust." Alice wiped her hands. "The only thing moving this car is another tow truck."

Violet walked around to stand beside her. "How would you feel about a bus?"

"Driving one?" Alice questioned.

"Well, you wouldn't drive it, you'd be a passenger." Vi held up the phone screen to show the image of a bus schedule.

"I would feel strongly *against* bussing to your aunt's house." Alice waved to fan the rising smoke. "I don't like buses."

"I understand that, but the other option is to wait for our buddy Ricky to come with a flatbed and bring us his twenty-five-year-old Buick Regal."

Alice turned, resting her weight on the front of the Fiat. "He's two hours away. That means we wouldn't see PB or the roller derby team tonight and we'd need to find a hotel."

PB, known as Stacey to the rest of the world, was Alice's close friend and the third partner of their former outdoor-adventure business. Alice shortened the nickname for the woman absolutely obsessed with perfecting her own grandmother's mulberry-jam recipe. As a joke on the trail, Alice sang a childhood song about peanut butter and jelly sandwiches, and for the last twenty years the nickname PB stuck like the gooey rehydrated combination they all craved mid-hike. Coincidentally, Stacey held the jammer position of her roller derby team so everyone referred to her as PB. Well, everyone but Violet.

"I think Stacey will understand once you tell her what happened to Bess."

Alice thought about the trip, about finding a single night hotel room and cramming herself and the Yule log tote onto a cross-country bus. "How would the bus situation work?"

Violet's shoulder rested against her wife's as they leaned together to look at the phone. "The station is about seven miles from here."

"We could walk that in an hour and a half. After PB's, when would the bus arrive at Auntie's?"

Violet scanned the information on the screen. She waved her phone in frustration. "With this route, just in time for the Solstice celebration, but we have to walk seven miles and take two buses to get to Stacey."

"Maybe PB could come get us," Alice suggested. "She's a little more than an hour moving in the right direction, and that would eliminate time wasted waiting for transfers at the stations."

While Violet called Stacey, Alice called their new best friend Ricky at Happy Car Rental to arrange for the pickup and tow-away of the Fiat. He offered the use of his personal car again but they declined. Once they reached Stacey's place, they would work out the rest of their route to Aunt Eunice's.

"Thanks, Stacey. Yes, we'll be ready and Alice will definitely take you up on a beer and burger for dinner this evening." Violet disconnected the call and turned to listen to her wife's refusal of the Buick once more.

"So Ricky was tons of fun." Alice slid the phone into her back pocket. "He said just leave the key in the glove box, we could also leave the snack cooler since it's mostly empty and he'll put it in Bess's back seat, but definitely lock the car."

"How's Bess?" Violet knew her wife would have asked, and hoped that maybe their freshly-repaired Outback would arrive on that flatbed and all would be right with the traveling world.

"Six feet over and getting an engine and frame check." Alice dropped the hood on the Fiat. "How is this our trip?" She walked to the trunk of the car and opened it.

"I'm not sure how to answer that."

"Maybe don't." Alice waved at the continued mist rising from the car. "What did PB say?"

"Stacey's such a sweetheart." Violet smiled. "She's actually in the area running an important errand. A surprise for us, she said, so she'll pick us up at the gas station across from the first bus stop."

"We should get moving."

"Perfect timing, though." Violet bounced on her feet. "Maybe this trip will turn around after all?" The peppy enthusiasm in her voice was endearing and another reason why Alice adored her wife.

Alice raised a hand, her fingers twisted together. "Fingers crossed."

"You know… we could walk and talk and snack on the celebratory picnic. It'll make the time go faster." Violet lifted her suitcase from the trunk, helping Alice with the tote.

Alice nodded. "That sounds perfect and since I won't be driving for a while I might pop the cork on our wine. PB won't mind." She draped the grocery bag over Violet's arm, removing the few items left in the cooler. It would be a trick to shoulder the Yule log container and sip a collapsible cup of wine but this day needed a bright side, even if it was the contents of a pricey bottle of Merlot.

"Stacey would absolutely love that you drank her wine if it takes the edge off this hike." Violet picked up her booted foot. "I wish I had better hikers on."

"Me too, but we've walked in worse." Alice set the tote in the grass and removed the multitool from her hip. Without looking, she opened the corkscrew feature. This knife was always with her. It was one of her favorite tools and the first gift Violet had given to her. Original Leatherman tools were difficult to find, and this one, with its nicks and scratches, was a replacement for what was lost during that first hiking trip together.

"We have definitely walked in worse." Violet passed the bottle of wine from her bag. She flipped the collapsible cups open and Alice filled each to the top.

"I can't believe we're hiking alongside a highway, sipping wine with a plastic container of Yule log." Alice took a cup and tapped it against her wife's. "Happy anniversary, my love. Thanks for giving me the best and weirdest life."

"Even though I bashed Bess, and we're walking seven miles?"

Alice nodded. "Yes, love. Even though you bashed Bess and we're walking seven miles."

# CHAPTER SIX

"How can it be raining?" Alice wiggled the cork into the bottle and passed it back to Violet.

Because a lifetime with Alice made Violet a planner, and she hated getting wet, Violet had a raincoat in her suitcase. The suitcase was waterproof—that is, until she opened it to take the raincoat out. "Do you want the meteorological explanation of rain or the weather-app forecast from my phone?"

They were standing beneath a tree alongside the highway, an absolute no-no during a rainstorm but there was no shelter that either of them could see.

"Since both of those forecasts said partly cloudy and a fifteen-percent chance of rain, I think they can both bite me." Alice raised the tote to balance it on top of her head, which was not going to keep any part of her dry. Her boots sloshed. Her pants clung to her legs and, at this point in the walk, there was nothing dry.

"It could be worse." Violet was going to be a ray of sunshine in this storm no matter what level of discontent her wife took on.

"Wait, what? Are you summoning hail now?" Alice joked as she heard the distinct rev of an engine coming up behind them.

"Slide over for the car, love, and watch that," Alice directed and they stepped away from the huge puddle as the car drove through it.

"Good call," Violet said.

A mile further down the road, they didn't have time to avoid the huge splash made by a passing truck. The horn blared as Alice dropped the Yule tote and shielded her wife from the splash of water.

"So chivalrous." Violet kissed her wife.

"I'm not sure that's the case since we're both drenched. Too bad the days of hitchhiking are over."

The next driver actually honked a horn to move them off the gravel and into the taller, unmowed grass.

"Are we there yet?" Alice joked.

"I sure hope so."

They heard a group of motorcycles long before they passed in a long line and Violet lost count at twenty.

Alice sighed, thinking how quickly they could get to the station to see their friend if the three-wheeled cycle she'd spotted had stopped.

"Are you thinking what I am?" Violet asked, after a few minutes of walking.

"If you were trying to summon that three-wheeled cycle to stop and pick us up, then yes. I was thinking that and I wish you had Eunice's Pagan summoning abilities to call that three-wheeler back. I'm going to call it Pagan pop."

"Pagan pop. That's cute and I'm giving it a try right now." Violet closed her eyes to concentrate and, seconds later, the mist of rain turned into a heavier sprinkle.

"Uh Vi, not a rain chant." Alice shifted the tote to her shoulder.

"It's not a rain chant. I was just saying, who wouldn't pull over to help two hot chicks?"

"A bunch of water-soaked riders on bikes trying to get out of the rain?"

"Oh, but look at us." What an odd sight they were, schlepping along the roadside, drenched from the rain, dragging a suitcase, a grocery bag of wine and a plastic tote holding a festive Yule log. Violet turned around to face her wife. Alice was soaked from head to toe, fighting to keep the longer hair on the top of her head from causing a river of water to flow into her eyes. The contoured top of the tote was holding just enough water to spill a few ounces if it tipped forward or backward. She appreciated the sacrifice Alice was making at that moment. "I'd stop for you in a heartbeat." She waited for her wife to get close enough so she could kiss her.

"If only I had a motorcycle, I'd take you for a ride." Alice set the tote on the ground. She took Violet into her arms, feeling the squish of water as she hugged and kissed her.

"I think I'd rather—"

The rev of a motorcycle engine interrupted their playful exchange. The rider, dressed from head to toe in worn black leather, kicked the stand on their bike and cut the engine. "You look like you could use some help." A second bike pulled over, coming from the opposite direction to Alice and Violet.

"We had a little trouble with our car." Alice hitched her thumb back toward the abandoned Fiat.

"We're trying to get as close to the bus station as possible," Violet explained, a little flummoxed by the leather-clad people in front of her. Leather was definitely a plus on her hot-or-not list for sapphics.

The second cyclist cut their engine and flipped up the visor on their helmet. "I'm guessing that's your Fiat a few miles back?"

Alice groaned. "Yes, it's our pile-of-junk rental."

The riders looked at each other and back at Alice and Violet. "We were thinking we'd give you a ride to the next dry place if you're good on a bike?"

Alice stood a little taller. "We're great on bikes but this thing might be a problem." She tapped the tote with her foot.

The first rider removed their helmet, and a long dark braid fell down their back. They held out a hand to Violet. “Bernie Fitch, but you can call me Peaches.”

“Peaches?” Violet questioned.

“Long story to tell while standing in the rain. My girl over there is Rheanne and her old lady, Mel, should be coming around right about now.”

The rev of the three-wheeled cycle was heard before it was seen. Like some kind of magic, there were three perfectly leather-clad rescuers in front of them.

“You don’t know how much we’d like a ride out of this storm right now.” Alice picked up the tote to carry it to the three-wheeled bike.

“Is that their Fiat back there?” Melanie laughed, pointing between the two bikers.

“Sadly, yes.” Alice held out a hand in greeting.

“Tragic thing to drive a car like that with all that luggage.” Melanie kicked her leg over the bike to shake Alice’s hand.

Alice noticed the off-balance walk and the specialty fitted boot on Melanie’s foot. “It might be the worst rental car on the planet,” she joked.

“I’d say it is if you’re walking in the rain.” Melanie opened a side compartment and removed a large clear garbage-can liner. “Let’s wrap it in plastic and give it a strip of tape to keep it dry.”

It was a generous gesture, Alice thought as they added the plastic wrapping to their Yule log tote. Although she was sure it wasn't leaking, the seal of a storage tote was always unpredictable.

Together, Mel and Alice tied the tote to the back of the three-wheeled bike. "Helmet?"

Yes, please." Violet put on the open-face helmet Mel had in her side bag and got on Rheanne's bike. Alice got on behind Peaches, who offered a similar second helmet.

Alice closed her eyes to the hum of the bike's engine. The vibration against her body was a reminder of their riding days.

"Ready to roll?" Peaches yelled.

A bunch of leather-gloved hands gave a thumbs-up and moments later they left the puddles behind them.

It took only minutes to travel the last miles and Violet felt nothing but glee as they rolled into the parking lot across from the bus station.

"Thanks for the ride, Peaches." Alice reached into her wallet to offer payment for the help.

"Keep it. Pay it forward." Peaches revved the cycle engine. "I'm glad we could help."

Alice unloaded the tote and after a few short waves Peaches and her friends disappeared from sight.

"That was amazing." Alice kicked her foot against the plastic-wrapped Yule tote. The motorcycle ride had been short but was enough to make her feel a bit nostalgic as they settled under the canopy behind the truck stop and visitor center. A gentle mist of rain began again.

"You miss riding?" Violet squeezed her wife's hand.

"I miss that feeling of moving fast and being right on the edge of control."

"That's my gal."

Alice opened the snack bag. With a flip of her wrist, she extended the collapsible cups. "How about another try at this wine?"

"We're going to drink it all." Violet wiggled the cork from the bottle and filled the cups.

"PB won't mind," Alice said.

Violet capped the bottle. "Only because there's a second one."

"She'll never know there were two." She touched her glass to Violet's. "Cheers, love."

# CHAPTER SEVEN

"The wine's gone." Alice tipped the bottle over her empty glass. They'd stretched out in a tiny patch of grass after the rain ended. The truck stop's lookout point had a gorgeous view of the mountains, which was why Violet, in her most wifely way, had encouraged Alice to sit in the wet grass. Selfies were a must-have in the moment because no one would believe the misadventure this trip had morphed into. They were making the best out of being stranded. Who could judge them for opening the second bottle of wine?

"Good thing you weren't thirsty, love." Violet snickered as she wiped at the stain on her wife's pants.

"Very good thing, I suppose, since my collapsible cup fell over three times and now the ants are getting drunk on a rather nice second bottle of Merlot." She flicked the cup with her finger. "They should call them tip-able cups instead of collapsible."

"They're more novelty and probably not for wine in a rainstorm." Violet leaned in for a kiss. "Happy anniversary." Her pivot spilled what was left of her wine.

Alice's forehead touched her wife's. "The happiest, all things considered, and there've been a lot of things in the last twenty-four hours."

"But we're here. Still motoring toward Auntie's house."

"Still motoring on, if you consider wine in the rain at a truck stop motoring."

They held hands, one leaning on the other for support as they watched cars drive in and out of the parking lot.

"It's probably weird, but I kinda like this," Violet whispered.

Alice's body shook with a rumbled laugh. "Baby, weird and us, we go hand-in-hand." Her wife startled at the sound of a semi horn. In the half-hour since Peaches and her gals dropped them off, they'd heard a ridiculous amount of horns and whistles while sitting in their grassy picnic spot. "We've done some things that don't even come close to how tame it is to sit in a truck-stop picnic area with a bottle of wine."

"Two bottles." Violet held up two wiggling fingers. "And I'm not sure we drank half a bottle between us, with all the spills."

"It could be more romantic." Alice rested her back against the plastic-wrapped tote.

"Yeah, it could be." It was a testament to their resilience, this mutual adoration born from rocky beginnings.

Alice closed her eyes, shaking her head as a different echoing car horn interrupted their tender moment. This one, like a toddler with a plonking drum kit, was more obnoxious as the pulsating beeps played an obvious tune.

"Stacey's here," Violet said as she covered her ears to block the sound that wouldn't stop.

"Holy shit with the horn. She hasn't changed a single bit." Alice stood to wave, toppling what was left of their liquid picnic. Violet picked up the cups and the bottles as Alice walked across the grass to greet their friend through the open car window.

"You're going to wake the neighbors," Violet yelled. The bottles clanged inside the bag as it hit the barrel of the garbage bin.

"Waking the neighbors is what I live for," Stacey yelled, sinking her elbow onto the rubber trim of the open driver's window. "You look like a sack of wet dogs."

"Wow, wet dog sack," Alice bit back. "Nice to see you, too, PB."

"Yeah, yeah." She hit the lock button on her car doors. "Are you bitches ready to roll?"

Alice stared at the car, eyeing up the magnet stuck to the driver's door: the swirling letters, anchored by skate wheels, transforming into a ribbon of rainbow colors screaming out of a drag performer's painted face. "Whore Moans." Alice couldn't hold her laughter as she read it aloud.

"That's the team name. It's so good, right?" Stacey shifted into park and hopped out of the car as the bright yellow Yaris lurched back and forth from the action.

Violet looked at the magnet. "Whores?" she questioned.

"The team is made up of a lot of different professionals," Stacey replied.

"PB, that's the best name for the queerest bunch of people on wheels. I love it." Alice threw her arms around her friend, giving her a giant squeeze and lifting the smaller woman off the ground. Unsatisfied her friend wasn't as wet as she was, she gave her another squeeze.

"Put me down, you brute. I'm all covered in Al glop."

Alice dropped her, and before Violet could step in Stacey scooped her up and twirled her in a circle.

"You haven't changed a single bit, Stacey." Violet hugged her back as her feet settled in the gravel.

"Wet hugs for everyone. Why change? I like me just the way I am." Stacey's smile punctuated the statement as her arms shook off the rain-soaked hug. She slipped her hands in her pockets and surveyed their surroundings. Her forehead crinkled with confusion as she noticed the Yule log tote wrapped in plastic, with a suitcase and duffle bag on top. "What have the two of you fallen into today?"

"You wouldn't believe us if we told you." Alice sidestepped the puddle in the parking lot. "You got everything, Vi?" she asked.

Violet patted her pockets, checking for her wallet and travel essentials, and rolled up her rain jacket which was almost dry. "I'm good."

"Me too." Alice hoisted the plastic tote into the trunk of the Yaris, pushing aside roller skates, wheels, wheel-bearing boxes, and laces in every color imaginable that one would need to individualize their skates. She unfolded a crumpled, blood-red T-shirt, holding it up for Vi. "The artwork for the team is so good!"

Stacey's cheeks rose with a huge smile. "One of the team members is a graphic designer and drag performer, so we let them use all their genius for the team gear."

"Seriously amazing." Violet traced the name.

"Sick, right!" Stacey squealed.

"Never change, PB. Never change." Alice tossed the shirt on top of the skates, tucked the duffle bag and suitcase in, and closed the hatchback.

"Thanks for rescuing us," Violet said as she fastened herself in the back seat.

"For all the times your soulmate has saved my ass, this is the least I could do."

"Seriously though, PB. With this mini rescue-mission we might make it to Eunice's in time to celebrate Solstice with her."

"Maybe you should have flown?" Stacey turned the car around.

"*Apparently* there are rules about transporting wood across state lines," Vi explained.

"Is my stick-to-the-rules bestie breaking the law?" Stacey's attempt at acting surprised was accented with a toothy grin.

"I am not! That's why it is sealed in a tote. No air in, no air out, and Auntie gets her Yule log as specified."

"Such a rebel." Stacey checked the rear-view mirror.

"That's my wife. Plus, that thing is so saturated with essential oils no insect or tiny critter could survive," Vi added.

"So you're saying *don't open it*?" Stacey joked.

"Don't even sneak a sniff." Alice chortled. "Plus you'd have to break through that plastic wrap, and Peaches and her gals made it tight!"

Stacey raised a questioning eyebrow.

"Don't ask." Violet said.

Stacey didn't. Instead she asked, "So how is Eunice, anyway?" Stacey's driving was loose, weaving back and forth from center line to roadside gravel, teetering on the winning side of recklessness. In the passenger seat, Alice was on edge as she tried to settle in for the trip with a white-knuckled grip on the handle by her head.

"Auntie is wonderful. Still hosting celebrations, obviously." Violet pointed her thumb toward the rear of the car.

Stacey nodded toward the tote. "Looks like she might be handing that over to you two?"

"Just the Yule log, and it's been a real treat to haul that sucker around." For the first time, Alice felt the full impact of the moisture in her clothes. "Didn't make a very good umbrella either."

Violet chuckled. "Not much did."

The laughter that followed was rooted in a friendship history that included long hikes, wet weather adventures and mishaps that happened very much like their road trip.

The hour-long drive was a course through the hibernating December countryside. Violet was content to listen to Stacey tell Alice about the Whore Moans and the growing support for their roller derby community as the league assembled under an enthusiastic LGBTQIA+ umbrella.

"So Billie, their derby name is Ber Sirk-her, they are nonbinary—the name suits them so hard—anyway, they took a huge tumble the night before last at an exhibition and recruitment event."

"Out for the season?" Alice asked.

"Billie?" Stacey laughed. "Not even out for the night, but they had to ride the bench for a bit for medical checks, concussion and all that bullshit, and they weren't happy. I got off the phone with them just before I picked up the two of you. They bent my ear about the concussion protocols for the entire drive."

"Billie sounds a little bit like someone I know." Violet looked at the reflection in the rear-view mirror, catching the knowing smile from Stacey.

"I don't know what or who you're talking about," Alice interjected.

"Yeah, yeah. You've played that butch card forever. We get it." Stacey waved off the comment, continuing, "So how did you end up broken down by the side of the road with biker chicks? What happened to our girl Bess?"

"*I* happened to Bess, and on our celebratory drive, too," Violet said, and Stacey raised a questioning eyebrow.

"Bess hit three-hundred-thousand miles on this drive so we stopped to commemorate the moment and someone forgot to put the car into park."

Stacey stopped at the four-way intersection. "You're shitting me?"

"I'm not, and it gets worse," Alice said.

"Wait." Vi held up her hands. "In my defense I was excited about *this* picture." She leaned between the seats to show Stacey the perfectly lit image of Alice frozen in time with the numbers of the odometer in the foreground.

"Bess really hit three-hundred-thousand miles. Look—at—her." Stacey whistled and checked the intersection. Not a car in sight, she pulled out onto the highway.

The adoration was sweet. "She's riding so well. Had her fifth set of tires put on for the drive." The way Alice spoke about Bess, the rest of the world might believe she was a twenty-year-old student heading off to college and not a twenty-year-old car.

Vi shook her head, eager to switch to a different subject. "What's going on with you, Stacey?"

"Same shit, different decade, I suppose. Got the league up and going."

"Yep, you said. What else?" Alice felt her wife's hand come around the seat of the car. The history was there, that day, and the scars each of the former members of the guide group carried. They never truly went away.

"I'm rolling all of my energy toward the derby league. It's good for me to stay active, and—"

"Yeah," Alice interrupted. "The leg must be good if you're the jammer on the team."

"The leg's been great since surgery. Only acts up if I'm on my ass too much."

Violet saw Stacey's focus shift down to look at her leg, and their eyes met on the return. "How are the nightmares?"

She shrugged. "They come and go, really. The counseling center keeps changing staff but they got a new chick who understands PTSD. She's former military. I like her. And my new meds help a lot. So does skating and putting the league together." She looked at Alice. "What about you and Vi?"

Alice shrugged.

"We're about the same," Violet answered.

"We have to go on living," Alice said, and the silence that followed was a statement about their past.

"Time helps a bit." Stacey's voice startled Violet.

"Speaking of time," Alice said, "we stopped at the national park and ran into Britt."

The information brought the car to an abrupt halt as Stacey pulled over. "No shit?"

"She's a park ranger," Violet shared with an apprehensive smile. "And she seems really happy."

Stacey shook her head, focusing closely on the carless highway ahead. "I don't think I could ever guide in that place again."

"She's the absolute bravest of us all," Alice added. "And if it wasn't such a deep part of me, I could understand. It's different for each of us."

"Yeah, it's different," Stacey whispered. They sat alongside the road for a long time, Stacey trying hard to push down her feelings. "She's a ranger. That means she can shoot and drive."

"Yep, and also hire the worst rental car on the planet," Alice joked, and it was enough to break the tension of the moment.

"You should call her." Violet reached forward to rest a hand on Stacey's shoulder.

Stacey's tear-filled eyes focused on Alice. "You know you're the glue, right?"

"I know I'm the glue that keeps us all together, and Vi's right, you should call her."

# CHAPTER EIGHT

Violet and Alice weren't sure what to expect as they pulled into the parking lot of the warehouse space Stacey called home.

"I'm excited to see the place." Alice had watched the view transition from their countryside drive, through residential subdivisions, until they turned off to enter a rundown industrial-park district.

"I'm excited for you to see it." Stacey's hands shuffled across the steering wheel. "I hope you love it as much as I do."

The building stretched for a city block, nearly three-stories high but much of it rough around the edges. Mismatched fencing surrounded what must have been a factory in the early 1900s. The project was a work in progress at the very best but it was also clear that many hands were part of the improvements being made.

"Home sweet home," Stacey proclaimed as she hopped out of the driver's seat to open the locked gate.

"You live in the warehouse?" Alice asked, leaning out the window.

Stacey keyed the lock on the twenty-foot-high aluminum-panel door and pushed it open wide enough for the car to pass through.

"There are about twenty of us living here." Stacey jumped into the driver's seat and drove the car through. The warehouse was massive, large enough for huge passenger planes to fit inside.

"How did you manage this?" Violet rolled her window down and she stuck her head out far enough to see the rows of tiny houses built along the stretch of the outer walls.

"Twenty people, professionals, working full-time jobs in the city, for the most part." Stacey pulled her car into the spot marked with a sign reading 'Jammer'. "I secured the building with a chunk of my malpractice settlement from the…" She paused. "Ya know." She patted her thigh. "Misty, she lives in that green house there." She pointed to the tiny home three buildings from the first row. "She's a professional grant writer. She found a couple of grants from the government to improve industrial sites like this. Without her contribution, it wouldn't be this glamorous." She chuckled.

"Misty, huh?" Alice harassed her friend. "What else does she contribute to?"

"My happiness?" Stacey didn't try to hide her smile. "You're not the only one who gets a happily ever after."

"That's sweet, Stacey," Violet said.

"It's mushy gushy," Alice teased, "and I can't think of a more deserving person. Will we get to meet her?"

"It depends?" Stacey was quick to say.

Violet patted Stacey's shoulder. "Don't worry, I'll make sure Alice doesn't scare her away."

"Misty is pretty hard to scare."

"I like her already." Violet chuckled.

Stacey turned to look at her friends with a vulnerability the rest of the world rarely saw her express. "I like her a lot."

Violet opened her door, mostly because she wanted to hug her friend, but when she stood in the parking lot the scene took her breath away. "Wow, you've made a tiny city inside here?" Vi's mouth fell open.

"Cool, right?"

"Very," Alice said as she exited the car to follow her friend.

"We set up a derby ring on the other side of that barricade." Stacey pointed to the reinforced wall surrounded by chain-link fencing. "That way, when we have an event, the village is kept safe from unwanted visitors."

Before Alice could ask a question about how they kept stray humans away, two thick, brown, short-haired dogs circled around the hip-high wall dividing the car parking from the entrance to their tiny home living space.

"Meet Ben and Jerry." Stacey dropped to one knee to welcome her dogs. "Al, come here and let them get to know you."

Alice stepped in first.

"Ben, he's mostly pit but I think he's also part Pooh Bear because he loves to stick his head inside everything. Thinks he's finding honey or something."

"Hi, Ben." Alice held her hand for him to sniff. After a few seconds of wet-nose scrutiny, the animal gave an approving lick.

"Violet, you should come in, too."

Vi squeezed in between her wife and Stacey, but Ben was fast to approach and tangle himself against her calf.

"I think Ben approves of your choice in life partners, Al."

"Thanks for your approval, Ben."

The dog pushed against Violet until she lowered herself to sit on the ground. Jerry, the pit bull with a wild mane of fur around his neck, crawled like a soldier on his belly until his nose was beneath Vi's hand.

"I guess the boys have a new best friend," Stacey joked as she stood.

"You've got great taste in women, boys." Alice rubbed their heads before standing. "This is an amazing setup, PB."

"The village is a safe little city for us, and yeah, it is pretty amazing."

"So you built your next adventure from the ground up." Alice threw an arm around her friend and they walked together toward the row of tiny houses.

"I'm really proud of it and for the most part we live an easy and simple life. If someone finds a friend or takes in a person in need we put them in a vacant tiny house and if they're a good fit we invite them to stay."

"The world could use a few villages like yours," Vi said. She followed with a frolicking pit bull at each hip.

"From your mouth to my next benefactor's ears."

They spent the next hour walking through the row of tiny homes, most the size of short shipping containers. There were four twenty-foot containers stacked like building blocks with scaffolding and staircases attached.

"What's that monstrosity?" Alice asked. "Looks like a good challenge to climb."

Stacey laughed at the rightness of the guess. As they walked around the opposite side of the structure, they could see the belaying ropes and handhold anchors on the wall's surface.

"That's amazing." Violet laughed.

"Like I said before, I'm fine as long as I keep my body moving." Stacey pointed at the wall. "And that keeps me moving."

"Can we climb?" Alice walked closer, tugging on the rope anchored to the floor, mesmerized by the possibility. She hadn't climbed in days, which felt like forever to her.

"Any time you want." Stacey pointed to the end of the stacked containers. "That one's a 6a. A great challenge for almost everyone here. Most of the village is still working on the fives over there." Violet and Alice understood the grading system of rock-climbing walls.

Alice's eyes glazed as she studied the hand- and foot-hold positions, making the experienced climber hungry for the challenge. "I need to hit that six." Alice raised her hands, floating hooked fingers from side to side, following the path of the holds anchored to the wall.

"Maybe next visit, love," Vi leaned in to whisper in her ear. "We've got a roller derby match to watch and I'd kinda like to change out of these damp clothes and not watch you two dangling from ropes."

"She'd be on her own today. I've got to save it for the match tonight," Stacey said.

As disappointed as she was, Alice was experienced enough to never climb without a partner. "Next time for sure," she said. "How 'bout you show us the rest of the village?"

"I'd love to."

The tour was short as they walked past the tiny homes. Each had a level of individuality that was obvious from the designated walkway path they followed. Stacey's wasn't the largest but it was definitely the most colorful.

"The orange suits you, PB."

"I know, right!" She pushed the front door open. "Welcome to my humble abode."

~~~~~~~~~~~

"Too bad she had to run off."

"It's a big night for her," Violet said as she pushed her suitcase closer to the bed. "She's excited we're here and maybe we'll get to meet Misty."

"I'm so curious." Alice unzipped her duffle bag. "Shit, my clothes are soaked."

Violet opened her suitcase on the floor to a similar experience. "Mine aren't soaked but they're definitely moist."

Alice slid the curtain covering the small closet. "There are four hangers, perfect."

"Did you hear me say I was moist?" Violet held up her dress, drops of water falling as she snatched the hanger from Alice.

Alice's mouth opened but no words came out.

"That's what I thought." She tapped Alice's chin to shut her mouth.

For the next few minutes they draped and strategically placed their clothes on every available piece of furniture in the tiny home. "It looks like a tornado flew through," Alice joked.

"A moist tornado?"

"Violet, you're—"

"I'm moist, Alice." Violet had stripped down to her matching bra and shorts. She stood in the doorway holding a compact hair dryer in her hand. "Off with your clothes, woman."

"Are you about to do something naughty with me?" Alice peeled her T-shirt over her head.

"I'm about to dry your shirt." She waved the hair dryer. "If that gets your engine revving, you can blow on me next."
~~~~~~~~~~~

"Violet Hadley-Crest." Alice's pants dropped to the floor. She chuckled when the solid objects in her pockets made a loud thunk. "Are you propositioning me right here in this tiny home with a blow-dryer in your hand?" She moved within arm-length of her wife.

"Maybe I am." Violet clicked the dryer on to fan her face. "And?"

"Maybe I can do something about whatever got you so moist."

~~~~~~~~~~~

Just before sunset, Alice and Violet wandered from the tiny home. "Feeling better?" Alice hooked Violet's belt loop to tug her close.

She tucked a hand in Alice's back pocket as they walked. "I am feeling so much better."

"And the moisture situation?"

"I think you took care of that, too."

Alice raised her eyebrow. "You think?"

"You can check, but it'll have to wait 'til later."

"What has to wait til later?" Stacey jumped out at them.

"None of your business," Alice said.

"It's a sex thing." Stacey smacked her friend on the back and Violet's cheeks flushed. "It *is* a sex thing!"

"Knock it off, PB," Alice defended her wife.

"It's fine, honey. Maybe we can meet Misty and return the harassment." Violet teased.

"And we're moving on," Stacey redirected, leading them to the roller derby arena. The fenced-in space was urban grunge at best, with mismatched chain-link and scrap-welded barriers
~~~~~~~~~~~

guiding spectators to the bleacher-bench style seating. Alice loved everything about the village's contribution to roller derby. The open ceiling looked like a web of pipe and wire tangled together to create pulsating lights connected to a decent sound system.

"This is going to be so great. I'm glad we made it here in time to watch." Alice squeezed Violet's hand.

"I didn't know Stacey had the focus to build something like this. It's wild," Vi said, half joking because it was a conversation they'd had while planning to meet Stacey but the description didn't do the village justice.

"I'm so happy for PB. I honestly don't care what she's doing so much as I want her to be successful, however that works out. Oh and obviously I want her to win." She winked at her wife.

People began arriving for the 7pm match. Alice enjoyed watching the diverse crowd of spectators mingle in. More than half wore the blood-red Whore Moans T-shirts and Alice swore she'd go home with one for herself and Vi, and she'd get the most rainbow-soaked shirt for Aunt Eunice. The DJ was on point, rousing the crowd into a chant for Stacey's team, the music raged with hard bass pulsing like a heartbeat against the steel barricades.

Alice stood chanting, "Whore Moans! Whore Moans!" She pumped her fist to the beat of the crowd. Announcements interrupted the music and asked all attendees to settle around the oval flat track.

From their seats, Alice and Violet could see most of the action. There was an apparent loyalty split between the crowd rooting for the Whore Moans and the other team drenched in black with huge flaming gold and orange letters dripping their team name, Hot Wheels.

The teams took turns skating the track to warm up, and before long the referee stepped out and blew the whistle. The ten skaters huddled together until the player with the red star on her helmet zipped past the clump. From Violet's perspective, the players bumped into one another, hips dipping and arms flailing as the skaters looped around, lap after lap. Violet had no idea who was earning the points or how, only that—from the numbers on the scoreboard—the Whore Moans were leading by fifteen points.

Al leaned close to Vi's ear. "I can't believe how exciting roller derby is. We need to do this more often."

"I guess I'll add roller derby to the list of new adventures my wife loves that I'll never fully understand?" Violet chuckled and winced when she saw their friend hit the surface of the track. "But only as a spectator." She squeezed Alice's hand.

Alice screamed as Stacey slid across the track on her knees before skipping up to her skate wheels to sneak by an opposing player. "Just as a spectator. There's no way I want to hit the floor like that."

"I think you could handle it." Vi nudged her wife with her butt. "But bleacher seats will work fine for me."

"Oh!" Alice stood as Stacey bumped into the pile, landing hard on her ass. "Maybe I could handle it, but my ass hurts just watching that. I don't know if I want to ice my ass anymore."

"Yeah, I kinda like warm Alice ass."

"Uh huh." Alice leaned closer to whisper, "You can have some of this later."

"I'll hold you to that—" Violet gasped as the Hot Wheels team's jammer took a hard hit. "Oh, that looks like it hurts."

The rest of the match was much of the same. Piles of skaters clumped like rugby players, moving around the track until the jammers broke free to score.

At the end, the Whore Moans won by a dozen points, and the team celebrated with drinks and food in the village courtyard.

"Pretty great, eh?" Stacey slid two drinks across the table to her friends. Her cropped hair was a sweaty mess but the joy in her eyes was unmistakable.

"Ridiculously so." Alice tipped her glass to tap Stacey's.

"Skates for you next visit, then?"

Alice shook her head. "Not in your life. That last hit you took is definitely going to leave a mark and I don't want any part of it."

"You'd make a great jammer if it didn't require wheels," Vi said.

"Exactly! Next visit, I'll cheer from the bleachers, just like I did tonight."

That debate settled, Alice turned her attention to the climbing wall behind them. "I know it's not exactly The Project in Sweden, but I really need to hit that wall right now."

"Yeah?" Stacey guzzled her drink and slapped her empty glass to the table.

"Oh *hell* yeah!"

Violet shook her head. "You two should not—"

"We're doing it." Alice chased after Stacey who was already unlocking the equipment cabinet.

"Don't poop the party, Vi!" Stacey didn't turn around, knowing exactly how Violet stood—hand on hip, chin out in her 'you'll regret this' stance. Stacey and Alice did stupid shit.

It was the love language between the two, and Violet was powerless once they set their minds to a task.

"You don't have any of your gear," Violet said.

"Oh, come on. Al could climb in bare feet," Stacey said. The use of the short version of the name made Violet double down on squashing their love language session.

"Twenty years ago she might have, but not today." Violet tugged her wife's arm. "This is not a good idea."

The giggling grin that stretched Alice's face would not submit to Violet's charms. "It'll be fine. We climb all the time." She stepped into the harness, threaded, buckled and double backed the straps over her hips and around her waist.

Violet flashed back twenty years to the impressive musculature of Alice's thighs hidden beneath the denim and wasn't shy about enjoying the memory.

"Like what you see?" Alice wiggled her eyebrows. Her hands moved in fluid motion as she tied in with a perfect figure-eight knot.

"No," Violet said, pulling the tail end of her wife's rope.

"Yes, you do." She wrapped her arms around her wife's waist, sandwiching Violet's hands between them.

"You're so stubborn."

Alice chuckled. "I've heard that somewhere before." She kissed her wife on the forehead.

"Oh my gosh, will you two just get a room!" Stacey clipped the Grigri belay device onto her harness and pulled up the slack in Alice's rope.

"Uh huh. We're gonna get one of your rooms right after I kick this wall's ass."

Before making another move, Alice checked Stacey's gear, and Stacey checked Alice's. "After everything we've been through, I better know how to tie *this* knot," Alice joked.

"I trust that I taught you well."

Violet shook her head. The two of them knew better than anyone what that safety check meant.

"You on?" Stacey asked.

Alice looked up at the face of the wall. "I'm on." There was no hesitation in her voice and she said. "Climbing."

"Climb, Al." Stacey anchored herself in place. "Just climb."

# CHAPTER NINE

"Not the smartest thing I've ever done." Alice cradled her left wrist against her chest as she popped a pill into her mouth. The urgent-care doctor was nice, but scolding, and if Stacey had been in the room there definitely would have been sparks flying. The strongest bond after nearly thirty years of friendship between Stacey and Alice was stretching their climbing limits.

"The doctor said to take both for the swelling." Violet turned the blister pack sample over, pointing at the second tablet.

"One is fine. It's not that bad." Alice downplayed the pain but it was obvious by her sausage-sized fingers that the swelling hadn't slowed.

"You know I fall in love with you all over again when you make reckless decisions like you do." Vi hit the lever on the door to exit the clinic.

"Don't say it." Alice tore at the velcro to loosen the wrap around her wrist.

"No?"

"Vi, I get it, I'm not twenty-five anymore but I climb enough to know I should have made that hook." The throbbing in her wrist was almost as painful as the embarrassment of spraining it.

"Your hips weren't twisted."

Alice shook her head, knowing her wife was absolutely right.

"And the foothold was off, too."

"I'm not sure what deity I pissed off on this trip, but it would be great if it could finish fucking up and we could enjoy the rest of our exciting journey to Eunices's," Alice shouted to the sky.

"There is a bright side." Vi waved at Stacey as she pulled up to the curb.

"Yeah, I'd like to know what that is."

Violet opened the door for her wife. "It's not broken and two weeks in a splint is easier than eight weeks in a cast."

"Hey, crash!" Stacey's arm was hooked over the back of the passenger seat.

"Can it, PB!" Alice bit back.

Stacey tapped the seat beside her. "Good to know it's not broken, but fuck, look at those sausage fingers." She made a flicking motion at the swollen digits, tempted to give them a hard tap.

"Don't you dare." Alice leaned away from the door so Violet could close it, moving her injury closer to Stacey. "It might be sprained but I can punch with my right fist just as hard."

"Your hips weren't—"

Alice raised her hand. "Twisted, right, I get it." She waved the splinted wrist. "Still, it was a great release."

"Would have been better if you actually caught the edge." Stacey laughed as she looked in the rear-view mirror. Violet was struggling to hide her laugh.

"No guts, no glory, right." Alice gave a toothy grin.

Violet shook her head. Twenty years earlier, she would have been the feral one of the bunch, reckless and free, but here she was, the sensible partner in the car full of wildings.

"Hell, yes! Absolutely no guts no glory," Stacey squawked.

"Right," Violet agreed. "She also needed a better warm-up."

"Can we just move on?" Alice was finished being harassed for reckless cocky climbing habits. She knew exactly what she'd done wrong in her quest to tackle the village's climbing wall.

"Yep, next visit you stay for the night and we do a full morning to sharpen up." Stacey said. "Deal?"

"Sounds like a great deal."

The tiny homes were dark as they pulled into the parking space in front of the village. "Do you need a *hand* with her?" Stacey stopped, giggling like a child as she let them out.

"I can manage." Alice raised a sausage-sized middle finger to her friend. "It's just a sprain, for crying out loud."

Violet leaned between the seats to kiss Stacey's cheek. "I've got her. She's no match for me tonight."

"Goodnight, then. I'll see you in the morning." She slipped a key into Violet's palm. "Call me if you need anything."

"We will," Violet said, waving as they walked up the path. "Are you tired?" she asked Alice as she unlocked the door.

"I could definitely sleep." Alice knocked the shirt off the chair as she walked around the high-top kitchen table.

"I bet this place is really cute when it's not covered with clothes." Violet picked up the shirt and draped it over the chair.

"Adorable." Alice's enthusiasm waned as she followed, kicking off her shoes in two steps. "Can we leave the clothes-tornado till tomorrow?" She entered the bedroom. "Ugh, more clothes."

"I'll take care of them. Are you going to bother with PJs?" Vi tugged a T-shirt from the hanger.

"How about my boxer shorts and something light?"

Vi hunted for the clothes, and passed a sleeveless shirt to her wife. "Get in bed, love."

Alice wriggled under the covers carefully to protect the splint on her wrist.

Violet tucked herself in around her wife and asked, "Is your arm okay like that?" She fluffed the pillow on their bed, happy for the privacy of the tiny home nestled at the end of the shipping container village. She took the big-spoon position for the night, her hand caressing tiny circles around the scar on Alice's hip.

"My arm is fine. I've had worse." Alice closed her eyes, fighting the movie-like replay of the past. Violet's fingertip against her hip rotated between the points where Alice had sensation and where she had lost it because of nerve damage. Inside and out, the scars were an unavoidable trigger like that.

Violet's hand stilled. "Climbing is always going to remind me of Britt."

"And of PB, too." Alice swallowed hard, struggling with her emotions. "Sometimes when I tie in, I can hear the sound of rocks crumbling. I look up and have that second of realization, that I was tethered with nowhere to run, and then I'm not."

Violet's breath was warm against Alice's neck as she whispered, "Your courage saved them."

"Your stubborn attitude did, too." Alice's heart ached from the memory. She pushed tighter into the curve of her wife's body.

"Do you need three minutes or do you want to talk to me?"

Alice's voice broke as she said, "It's been so long, but when the urgent-care nurse opened that cuff and wrapped it around my bicep it was like I was there again. The smell of disinfectant and the beeping of monitors."

"Our lives were in danger that day, love. It's always going to be a part of us." Violet didn't let go as her wife tried to pull away. "Stay here. Just let me hold you while you talk."

But Alice didn't talk for the longest time. Violet was patient. Their trust built over twenty years was stronger than any knot they ever tied.

"Animal attacks were always a vital conversation during every trip we guided," Alice began and Violet waited; she'd listened to this struggle hundreds of times and it never got easier. "Britt knew. PB knew, too, but we always thought it wouldn't happen to us because we were fast. We were good. We planned and prepared. We had a hundred trips between us without a single animal encounter."

"I know," Violet whispered.

"I never stop seeing the blood and you… what you did after all of your bitching and complaining. You were listening to every word when we lectured about first aid."

"You said a lot of things on that trail and I liked hating you almost as much as I loved falling in love with you."

Alice's body shook as her laugh transformed into tears and the only thing she could do was surrender to the safety Violet's arms created.

"There aren't any words I can say that will erase what happened to Britt or to Stacey or to you, but we've come out on the other side and so have they."

"We have... but I love climbing." Alice swiped her eye across the shoulder of her T-shirt. "I love it and I hate it and it's only sometimes that it hurts to need it."

"It wasn't your hips tonight, was it?"

"Fuck, woman. When did you get so damn smart?"

Violet's body trembled with a chuckle. "Right around the time some beautiful, burly woman made a play for me."

"Super smart that you grabbed her right up." Alice grinned.

"One of the smartest decisions I ever made," Violet whispered in her wife's ear, "but sweet talking me isn't going to prevent you from having to answer the question."

"I had a flashback. It was just for a moment when PB took up the slack. The clip hit against the Grigri and the pull on my harness. It was just enough to trigger that sense memory."

"And you saw the big cat?" Violet whispered.

"I saw it."

"And the tug made you feel what?" Her question was gentle because she knew exactly what her wife was about to share.

"It made me feel like I had to escape."

"Will you make a note to talk about it in counseling?" Violet's voice was so close to Alice's ear it made her shiver.

"I will."

"Good." Vi's arms flexed around Alice. "What else?"

Alice squeezed her wife's hand where it rested on her hip. "Britt."

"Mm-hmm."

The sound encouraged Alice to continue. "She wanted a different life."

"Yes, she did," Violet agreed.

There was no safer place to be than in the arms of a woman who'd proven her love time and again. "I want her to be happy."

"She knows."

Alice shook her head. "I think I need to tell her that."

"That's a good idea, my love, but not tonight." Violet pulled her closer. "Get some sleep now."

"Okay." Alice kissed the knuckles on her wife's hand before clutching them to her heart. "I love you," she whispered, and moments later her body relaxed into exhausted slumber.

"I love you, too." Violet closed her eyes, the minute-by-minute replay of that climb unfolding for her as if in real time: fingertips gripping stone, belay ropes tethering them together and the sound of that cougar as it tore at Britt's fighting hands. She remembered the blood, too—the increasing pool of red spilling against the sand- and pebble-covered ground as Alice threw her body between her climbing partner and the teeth of a wild animal. Clips and knots were meant to hold you in, no matter what.

No matter what.

She was wide awake for hours after Alice's breathing slowed, torn between their past and this present. According to years of therapy, their external scars were different, but their internal scars were so very much the same.

~~~~~~~~~~

Their morning walk from the temporary tiny home with an extremely soft bed to Stacey's home was short, but they enjoyed the village in the light of day. The steel and glass panels
~~~~~~~~~~

at the highest point of the exterior walls let in the morning light as if the barriers didn't exist.

"What an amazing place they're building," Violet whispered.

"PB always had larger-than-life dreams." Alice kissed the knuckles on Violet's hand before snugging it on her hip. "This doesn't surprise me at all."

As they approached the tiny home, the front door opened with as much vigor as the blaring car horn during yesterday's parking lot pick up.

"Good morning, lovebirds." Stacey stepped out. "Come on in."

"Good morning," they said in unison as they followed their friend through the cute and simply-decorated tiny home.

"So here's my place."

Alice felt Violet's hand fall away as they wandered through the room. It felt large for what was once a shipping container. She heard Violet ask a question but the conversation faded, voices going dim as she noticed a picture on the wall.

It was her Extreme Adventure Group team—Stacey, Britt and Alice—their arms wrapped around each other as they stood atop their first sixteen-thousand foot peak. Alice's arm was flexed, holding a thumbs-up, while Britt pointed at her shirt that read 'race you to the top.' The smiles were the golden moment, frozen in time, captured by a camera they'd wedged on a pile of rocks.

"Cool, huh?" Stacey threw an arm over Alice's shoulder, interrupting the memory.

Alice resisted the temptation to hold the photo in her hands, and touched Britt's image in the photo instead. "The picture is unbelievably cool. Where did you find this?"

"When I moved my gear out of storage, the negatives were mixed in with a bunch of legal documents and medical records."

"Look at your baby faces." Violet tipped her head toward her wife's shoulder as she leaned for a closer look.

"Oh for shit's sake, we were such children," Alice whispered, but she could recall almost every step of that hike.

"This picture was supposed to be my big surprise yesterday," Stacey said. "I didn't get to frame it or wrap it but I was picking up a print of this for you when you called me." She handed Alice an oversized photo envelope. "I knew you'd want it as soon as you saw it."

Alice wiped her eye with the back of her hand. "Yeah, this is something." She didn't try to fight the tears. "Thanks, PB."

"It's an honor and the least I could do."

"You should send a copy to Britt," Violet suggested.

"That was also part of my plan."

The silence that followed was an unspoken reverence toward friendship, the long embrace of chosen family, and the enduring bond of surviving a tragedy. Stacey disappeared into the kitchen. Alice and Violet wandered in a few minutes later.

"So, how was the bed?" Stacey asked as she set two cups of coffee on the kitchen table.

"Better than that time we climbed in Yosemite and slept in that porta-ledge." They both laughed, understanding that although there was no fear of heights between them, there was always a healthy respect for the tether anchoring them to the side of a rock wall.

"Nothing like waking up dangling from a rope?" Violet joked. She'd never climbed the way that Alice and Stacey had, and was content with that omission from her history.

"I'll take a bronco over a cougar any time," Stacey half-heartedly joked, but none of them laughed. The reference to the violence of the wind acting on their porta-ledge style tent was nothing compared to the animal that left the four of them with a lifetime connection of layering scars.

"I'd have to agree," Alice said as her breath blew across the steaming mug of coffee. The silence that followed wasn't awkward as each put the memories of the past away for a while.

"Breakfast is never on the menu here but we can grab something on the way to the bus station," Stacey offered.

"That'll hit the spot just fine." Violet rested her arms on the tabletop as she let Alice and Stacey sort through their memories.

~~~~~~~~~~~

"Looking less like a tornado now," Violet said as she checked the dampness of her jeans before folding them into her suitcase.

"Can you slide this into the sleeve of your shell case?" Alice asked as they packed their bags. She held the envelope like a prized possession because it would always be that for her.

"Yep, put it in right here." Violet flipped the zipper flap, exposing the pocket. She met Alice's trembling hands. "You're managing all of this really well."

"Nah, I don't think so." Alice sat down on the bed with the deepest sigh. "It's been a lifetime, and I love PB, but the way we're connected now, it's hard to remember the way we were before." She picked at the velcro on her splint. "It's frustrating and I wish I could stop it."

"Trauma is never really gone, love."
~~~~~~~~~~~

Alice blew out a huge breath. "Yeah, don't I know it."

"No matter how you tear parts of yourself, and stitch them back together, they'll never be what they were."

"It's such bullshit."

Violet sighed. "One day you'll see Britt and Stacey, and it won't *only* be the damage, and you'll move on as the changed person." Violet knew what this was. She understood the guilt of surviving and 'what-ifs'.

Alice looked up at Violet. "They're both really happy."

"We're all really happy. Sometimes we need to remember, that's all." Violet stepped between Alice's knees, holding the woman close to her. "I love you. I've got you."

And Alice felt the truth in her words. If Violet said she had you, there was no safer place to be.

~~~~~~~~~~

"Pancakes and coffee," Stacey said, flipping her cup over. Her favorite diner was the greasiest spoon in town, and absolutely her style.

"What's your favorite item on the breakfast menu?" Violet asked the waitress.

"The pancakes," Stacey and the waitress said together.

"Pancakes for me then." She looked at her wife knowing she'd go for a lighter choice.

"Two eggs over easy and dry rye toast," Alice said as she flipped her mug over. "And coffee, please—just keep that coming."

Stacey handed the menus to the waitress. "Not much different, are you boss?"
~~~~~~~~~~

The comment, although innocent, created a sense of melancholy that Alice had not put away from the earlier conversation. The table fell silent as the waitress returned to fill their cups.

"Not much." Alice said.

~~~~~~~~~~~

After their simple diner breakfast, the trip to the bus stop was short.

"We're really going to take that?" Alice stared at the wheeled cart that Stacey had bungee-tied tightly under the plastic-bag-wrapped Yule log tote. A Whore Moans team sticker covered where the criss-cross of duct tape ran over the lid. It was a horrendous spectacle and Violet loved it.

"Hell yes, you're going to take that," Stacey said.

"Thanks for the ride, PB, and for breakfast." Alice rubbed her belly with her splinted arm before hugging her friend. "And thanks for the wheelie cart to haul our prize. I don't feel old *at all*."

"Happy to help, grandma," she said, and they laughed. "And Vi." She pointed at the tote. "Make sure you give your auntie all kinds of love from the team. Wish her a happy solstice from all the whores." She handed Vi a rumpled, rainbow team shirt. "Give her this."

Violet laughed. "She'll be very entertained." The front had the team logo and on the back were the initials 'PB'.

"It's my team shirt," Stacey said. "Don't worry, I washed it."

"She'll love it."

"You sure you don't want me to hang out while you wait?" Stacey asked.
~~~~~~~~~~~

Alice checked her watch. "It's just about an hour. We'll be fine. I'm sure there's a place for coffee or something."

"It'll be an adventure." Vi's suggestion was perkier than necessary and neither Stacey nor Alice believed a single word.

"Oh yeah, like that ride we took in Florida, right?" Stacey laughed. "That dude. Fuck, he was a menace."

Alice shook her head. "That dude was an idiot and could have killed someone."

"Wait, what?" Violet questioned. "Why haven't I heard this story?"

"You never told her the bus story?" Stacey rested her butt on the hood of her car as she settled in to share their story in the most animated way. "So we're coming back from a survivalist training event in the middle of nowhere Midwestern America."

"Missouri," Alice inserted.

"Whatever, we were in the sticks, and beefcake over there hadn't taken a proper shower the entire time because she wanted to 'immerse herself' in the wild." Stacey's quote fingers hooked in the air longer than necessary. The three of them knew how serious Alice was when she was guiding long trips. "So we get on this bus and sit ourselves away from the rest of the passengers because of stinky over there."

"We get it." Alice raised her middle finger.

"So what happened?" Violet was getting impatient as she reached to smother her wife's offending finger.

"Nothing, for the first few hours. Al and I slept mostly. But then this guy comes on at a remote pick-up point. Now remember, there are like thirty other empty seats on the bus, and this guy sits right in front of us."

"Not because he liked the back of the bus," Alice added.

"Right." Stacey raised her knuckles and they fist bumped. "Not even five minutes goes by before the dude proceeds to pull out a knife and threaten to rob us."

"On a bus?" Violet asked, confused.

"High as a kite, I shit you not." Stacey's arms waved wildly as she spoke. "I'm not sure what he was thinking, but this one," she pointed at Alice, "she leaps over the seat, full steam ahead, and decks the dude solid to the face."

"That's my girl." Violet patted Alice's hip.

"Yeah, a big hero," Alice added. "Two things happened simultaneously."

"Oh yeah?" Violet raised her eyebrow.

"Yeah," Stacey interrupted again, "that dude crumpled like an accordion." She smashed her palms together. "And the bus driver slammed the brakes so hard that Al ended up five rows forward with two bruised ribs."

"My hero." Violet batted her eyes, mockingly like a damsel being rescued.

"Hardly," Alice chortled. "That driver didn't move one inch until the cops came. We were taken off the bus and handcuffed for bullshit assault because the driver only saw me hit the dude."

"Did they arrest both of you?" Violet asked.

"You know her," Stacey hitched her thumb at Alice. "She sweet talked the cop, really played up the rib thing, and when they found the dude's knife they let us go."

"Yeah, in the middle of nowhere because they wouldn't let us back on the bus."

"Ha, that's kinda funny because we did almost the reverse of what happened to you today." Stacey laughed.

"You rented a car?" Violet guessed.

Alice nodded. "It cost a fortune back then. Well, it was a fortune to us because we didn't have much more than what fit in our packs."

"Man, I sure hope you have a better experience on the bus to see your aunt," Stacey added.

"Seriously." Alice looked up as a bus pulled into the station with number 212 on display. "I think that might be ours."

"That's cool." Stacey stepped closer to Violet. "You take care of this one." She punched at Alice who dodged the fist like a prize fighter.

"Don't you worry, Stacey, I'll keep her on the straight and narrow." They both laughed as Alice leaned away to question the comment.

"I have never been, nor will I ever be, straight and most definitely not narrow."

"Oh, right. I remember. I should keep you on the queer and wide."

"Queer and wide, that's right and never forget it." Stacey laughed as she moved her arms around Alice for a hug. "Love you," she whispered.

"I love you, too," Alice said a little louder.

"Catch you on the flip side." Stacey waved as she got in her car, honked hard on the horn and drove away.

Alice hovered as the bus driver loaded the plastic-wrapped tote strapped to a wheeled cart, the duffle bag and the carry-on suitcase into the luggage area beneath the passenger compartment. Hesitant to be a passenger, Alice was not looking forward to the ride.

*"Love you guys."* Alice read the text message from Stacey to her wife.

"We need to make sure to see her soon." Alice lingered outside the bus, resisting the climb up the narrow steps.

"Come on." Violet tugged her arm. "No one is going to come after you on the bus.

"Now you know why I like to be behind the wheel," she mumbled as she reached for the handle on the stairs.

"Don't worry, you'll be safe with me," the driver said as he waited to scan Violet's electronic ticket.

"I'll hold you to that." Alice showed him her phone, he scanned the ticket and she followed her wife to the third-row seats. "I can give up a little control, but there's no way I'm tempting fate by sitting back there."

"Maybe for once you'll be rested when we get to Auntie's and your wrist can rest, too." Violet patted the splint.

"Sleep while he drives?" Alice raised an eyebrow. "Not in all my years of owning a car—" She paused and Violet knew why.

"Bcss is finc."

A bobbing nod was all Alice could make as her arms crossed tight over her chest. For the next twenty minutes, she watched people find their seats.

"Your face is saying a lot right now." Violet bumped her wife's shoulder.

"Is it saying I don't want to be on this stupid bus?" Alice stared forward, her eyes never leaving the door.

"Baby, it's saying you don't want anyone else to be on this bus." She tugged Alice closer to whisper in her ear, "I know you like being the boss but what could go wrong now?"

Alice's eyes went wide. "Why would you say that?"

# CHAPTER TEN

Violet sat wedged against Alice's shoulder. It was the most comfortable she could get on the seat as the bus hummed along. The hazy film and scratches on the window tint prevented her from enjoying the beauty of the terrain, but progress toward Aunt Eunice's home was the goal, even if she'd watched their planned travel stops slip by on every highway sign. She gave up on the outside scenery and switched to the print version of their audiobook.

"You feel that?" Alice whispered over the top of her wife's head.

"Pothole." Violet didn't look up from the chapter. The horror house was speaking to the main character again, and she needed answers to the freaky plot.

Alice chuckled. "You say pothole every time. If this road had that many I think it would be dirt or gravel."

"Uh huh."

"Are you reading ahead?" Alice tipped the phone screen. "You *are* reading ahead."

"Of course I'm reading ahead." Violet pushed the phone against her chest. "They're detectives in a haunted house and the house is talking to them. I have to know why."

"And what's the answer?" Alice pushed the phone with her fingertip, curious too.

"I don't know." Violet grinned. "The author is still dancing around the explanation."

"Probably a murdered bunch of children," Alice guessed.

"That's what I thought, too," Vi agreed.

"It's a bouncing ball." Alice expanded her guess and Violet raised her eyebrow questioningly. "The thumping in the hallway. It's a children's ball bouncing."

"Spoiler alert!" Violet joked.

"Is it a spoiler if I'm guessing?"

Violet turned off the screen. "Uh, yes, it is."

The bus thumped over another mysterious pothole bump, but this time it felt different.

~~~~~~~~~~

*What could go wrong now?* Alice repeated Violet's bus station words over and over in her head as she pointed at the ground. "The bus has a fucking flat tire, Vi."

All of the passengers from the bus—Violet counted close to thirty—stood along the side of the road waiting near the luggage-compartment doors.

Alice couldn't help herself. She stepped closer to the driver and knelt down in the gravel beside him to look at the tire.

"Been driving for nearly thirty years, and I never caught a sidewall blowout like that." He kicked the rubber folding over the rim's edge.

"It really is a flat tire." Alice felt a twinge of pain as her wrist splint snagged on her pant leg when she stood.

"Yep, sure is, and as soon as the new bus gets here we can transfer all of you onto it and we'll get you back on your way to the train station." His words lingered as Alice tried to process their reality.
~~~~~~~~~~

"Train?" Alice huffed, and felt a hand come around to cover her mouth.

"We didn't book train tickets," Violet said with the sweetest voice.

"I'm just a bus driver. Train tickets are not something I can take care of. The new bus is headed north to the trains so you'll have to manage tickets in the station." It was clear he was confused as Violet dragged her wife away from him.

"Don't say anything to him." She moved her hand to point at her wife. "Don't!"

Alice glared.

"Refrain from speaking."

"Are you—" the hand pushed her mouth tighter.

Violet took a deep breath. "Flat tires happen. I know this is the last thing we need but technically we are still on schedule and we can both sleep on a bus or a train and it'll keep moving in the dark." She pointed to the sky with her eyes. "Do you see the dark coming?" Her hand fell away.

"I see the dark and I'll raise you a fucking flat tire!"

"Nothing we can do." Violet turned toward the replacement bus, taking in the half-sized vehicle that was more like a preschool-sized short bus. "Let's go get on it."

Alice stopped in front of the plastic-wrapped tote. It had been separated from the wheeled cart, which now lay across the top. "Uh, why's it taken apart like this?"

The new driver, half her height and seemingly twice Alice's age, stood beside the last bags, which happened to belong to Violet and Alice.

"These are yours?" he asked.

Alice's frustrated silence was obvious to Violet so she answered. "Yep, those are ours."

His boot tapped the Yule log tote. "Can't take that." He didn't elaborate as he held the suitcase and duffle bag up.

"What do you mean?" Alice asked.

"No room. You'll have to—"

Alice held up her splinted hand to pause the conversation. She took three deep breaths, grabbing precious seconds but wishing for minutes. "There's room," she said through clenched teeth.

"Thirty passengers, thirty places to sit, and your bags have to go on the floor."

"I'll hold it on my lap," Alice said.

He looked at the tote, sizing it up against the two of them. "Won't fit."

"We aren't leaving it behind," Alice and Violet said in unison.

"Suit yourself, but you get one seat and you have to figure it out, and we're leaving." His about-face was abrupt as he stepped to board the narrow staircase.

"He's so full of shit. This bus holds thirty-six people. It's like the one we used to transport hikers," Alice mumbled as she watched her wife struggle to turn the tote sideways on the cramped stairs. The driver's disapproving expression was not helping the situation. Alice glared at the duffle bag resting on the seat behind the driver, which had plenty of space for a Yule log tote and the detached, collapsible wheeled cart.

"You've got to be kidding me," Violet whispered as she took in the last open seat in the very back of the bus. The aisle was too narrow to carry the tote through, so she heaved it over her head, wishing Alice's brawn wasn't hindered by the splint as they bumped and twisted their way down the aisle.

"You got it okay?" Alice kicked the suitcase as she sandwiched the duffle and wheeled cart against her abdomen.

"I'm fine. It's just kinda—"

"Heavy." Alice supported the tote with her uninjured hand. "Sorry, love."

"We'll be okay." Violet made it to the back and dropped the tote on the floor between the grade-school style bench seats. "At least there's room under us for the bags."

"Right." Alice kicked the suitcase beneath their seat, pushing hard to wedge enough space for the duffle bag, wheeled cart and their feet.

"You can't leave it there." The driver's eyes were in the reflection of the rearview mirror, staring daggers at them. "You can't block—"

"The emergency exit!" Alice yelled. "I got it. I know. We just need another second."

The double doors of the bus squeaked as they closed. All eyes and attitudes fell toward their predicament with the Yule log tote.

"Is it going to fit?" Violet whispered as she wriggled closer to the wall of the bus.

"It has to." Alice wedged the bin across her lap, pinning the two of them in the least comfortable position. "How far away is the train station?"

Violet shrugged. "I have no idea, love."

"It's just over two hours," a child-like voice answered from the seat in front of them.

"At least it isn't too much out of the way."

Another voice laughed before adding, "Unless you were headed south."

Alice's forehead thumped against the plastic tote. They were definitely headed in the opposite direction.

~~~~~~~~~~~

"How's your ass?" Alice whispered the question through a snicker.

"Well, my right cheek is fine." Violet wiggled against the seat. "But my left cheek hasn't had feeling since we hit that massive pothole in the road."

"Don't get me started on the potholes in this area. Would you like to switch cheeks?" Alice slid to the side to relieve pressure, all the while keeping an eye on the driver. It had been nearly two hours since pulling away from their highway ditch, where the bus broke down, and she was counting the minutes until their arrival at the station.

"You know, this reminds me of my ride from the hotel camp to that first stop at the national park," Violet said, her voice low to keep the illusion of privacy. "You weren't on that transport, but Greta was funny."

"Yeah, she was. I thought you were spoiled back then."

Violet feigned shock. "And now?" She reached under the tote to touch her wife's hand.

"Oh, now I *know* you're spoiled, and that's the way I like you."

"Good to know." Violet's head fell against the padded seat back; she was perplexed by how six inches of padding could feel like a surface of rock.

Alice slid the tote to the floor, wedging it half in and half out of the seat so she and her wife could switch positions discreetly.
~~~~~~~~~~~

"That can't be in the aisle." The driver yelled, and almost every head turned around to look at the two of them in a half-bent low-hurdle to maneuver around the seat.

"We're switching positions," Alice yelled back. Before she could say, "It'll only be a second," the brakes squealed. Alice flew sideways and Violet jerked forward as the bus stopped. Their bodies slapped the seat back but Alice was quick enough to prevent her wife from tumbling down the aisle.

"Oh, geez, that's gonna leave a mark," the guy in front of them tsked in the worst Midwestern accent.

The driver stared up at them. "We'll get back to it as soon as you're seated and that thing is no longer blocking the emergency exit."

"You okay, love?" Alice cupped her wife's cheek.

Violet looked into her concerned eyes. "I've taken harder hits than that."

"And we don't have to pick rocks from your knees this time." Alice scooted in against the wall of the bus.

"That's when you fell in love with me." Violet smiled, hoisting the Yule log tote into the seat and threading herself behind it.

"No, you always think that, but it took longer." Alice tugged the tote so most of it rested on her thighs. "You were a real pain in the ass."

"I still am and I'll never say I'm sorry for it." Violet pecked a kiss on her wife's cheek.

"Baby, *that's* why I fell for you."

# CHAPTER ELEVEN

"Thanks for the delightful ride," Alice said as her hip bumped into the door of the bus. She had her duffle bag across her shoulder, juggling Violet's suitcase and the wheeled cart in her unsplinted hand. She could hear her wife knocking the seats as she navigated the narrow aisle. Violet was the last one to exit, neither of them caring how many knocks the foam-backed seats endured.

"Have a nice evening." The driver stood solidly in place, watching Violet squeeze past to make the sharp turn at the steps.

"Alice, hon, can you grab the other end?" Violet paused at the narrow doorway, which felt smaller than when they'd boarded.

Alice dropped the bags and kicked the wheelie cart to expand it, elbowing the door to open it fully. "Asshole," she whispered under her breath, certain this bus driver's attitude wasn't the norm and wondering why he had to go out of his way to make things so difficult. Together, they attached the plastic-wrapped tote to the cart. The Whore Moans sticker made Alice smile as they dragged themselves and their bags toward the sliding glass-panel doors.

The bus ride had not been comfortable or relaxing, which made them beyond excited to stand in the terminal and finally be off the bus. The train station was noisier than Violet expected for so late in the day. "I can't believe I'm so exhausted," she huffed.

"My right butt cheek is kinda numb," Alice joked, trying to adjust herself with their tote attached to the wheeled cart and their bags resting on top. It felt like a victory after their ridiculous bus ride experience but there wasn't time to enjoy a single moment. She settled her arm on the narrow counter under the ticket window and started talking to the agent on the opposite side of the plexiglass divider.

Violet was distracted, watching a line of people move up the escalator behind them, missing the conversation her wife was having with the agent.

Alice turned, looking over her shoulder to get her wife's attention. She repeated the ticket options available for the six-hour train ride to the station near Eunice's home. "Coach seats for two are a hundred or a bedroom is six."

"Six hundred dollars?" Violet nearly choked as she repeated the price.

"Yep."

"Or there's a mini sleeper, our roomette, for three hundred and eighty," the ticket agent said. "And you can check that as a suitcase." He tipped his pen at the Yule log tote strapped to the wheeled cart.

"Three hundred and eighty dollars?"

"Yes, Vi, *dollars*," Alice repeated, a little irritated by the experience and anxious to make the train which was arriving in fifteen minutes.

"The mini-sleeper roomette has a bed in it?" Violet asked. The station was a paperless venue and because she'd read the eBook on the bus, her cell phone wasn't charged enough to look at the website to make an informed decision about their seats.

"It has a fold out and a bunk," the ticket agent said. "It's the last one available for this route. You want it?"

Violet thought the cost was crazy. "No!"

"Yes!" Alice did not want another butt-numbing ride.

The agent raised an eyebrow at the conflicting answers.

"Yes, we want it," Alice said. "We can stretch out to sleep, and with those few hours we'll be rested and ready for Eunice."

"Okay, sold." Violet clapped her hands.

Alice chuckled, appreciating the response to getting a little rest. She tapped her credit card against the machine.

Violet leaned closer to the hole in the plexiglass barrier. "We've never taken a train. What do we need to know?"

"Download the app." The agent held up a code for her to scan. "It'll answer every question you have about being on board. It'll also keep track of the tickets I just emailed to you." He pointed at Alice but continued talking to Violet. "The train leaves from platform A, and you can queue up now. Staff will check your tickets and tell you which car has your room."

"That's it?" Violet asked.

"Someone will show you the facilities, and the dining car will be open 'til eight to accommodate the new passengers from this station."

Violet was about to ask another question when an announcement interrupted her.

"That's your train." The ticket agent pointed them toward the escalator. "Go up one level and they'll call for private-room passengers. Next, please." He dismissed them without another word.

"Uh, thanks," Violet said as she dragged the luggage cart toward the escalator. "Kinda rude."

"He's got tickets to sell, love." Alice downloaded the app to her phone and set up the account while they moved across the station.

Violet kicked the wheeled cart onto the escalator and they rode to the top. The second level was large enough to fit a train inside, and the line of passengers stretched the entire length.

"How many people do you think can fit on a train?" Violet asked.

Alice laughed as she pointed to the queue. "At least that many."

"Smart ass." Violent bumped her wife's hip and was about to respond when a voice came over the sound system for private-room passengers.

"That's us." Alice picked up the pace.

"Are you excited to ride a train?"

Alice turned around, her arms out wide as she proclaimed, "I love the train. I love, love, love, love, love the train. It's so lovely!"

"You're kidding me, right?"

Alice opened the ticket app on her phone. "I heard a little kid scream that, once. It was a little voice coming from a car on the train ride at a wildlife venue."

"That's really sweet." Violet smiled.

"That little girl *really* loved the train. I was trying to psych myself up for this ride."

"By being an eight year old?"

"Yep."

"Tickets, please." The attendant waved a hand scanner.

"For the two of us."

"You have a sleeper?" the attendant asked.

"Yes."

"Check your bags as you board and meet with Marcus. He'll help you during the ride." The scanner beeped twice. "Go down the escalator, follow the green line, and you'll be in car 3320."

The car number appeared on the app along with a pixelated scannable code. "It's kinda intimidating the way an app knows where we should go," Alice said.

"Technology is kinda cool like that," Violet said. "You should embrace it more."

"I still like what I can touch and feel." Alice picked up the duffle bag. "I trust my hands."

"I trust your hands, too." Violet winked. "I also don't mind a little bit of technology."

"That's why we're so perfect." Careful to cradle her arm, Alice tugged the handle of the wheeled cart, managing all of their bags.

"I am capable of helping, you know?" Vi stepped forward on the escalator.

"Doesn't mean you have to." Alice followed, turning to balance the wheeled cart and the suitcase on top of it.

"One handed burl, I like it."

Alice leaned to whisper in Violet's ear, "I knew you would."

They stepped onto the concrete landing as their train pulled into the station. The attendant stopped them from wandering toward the front of the train.

"Which car?" She raised her eyebrow as she noticed the plastic-wrapped tote on the wheeled cart. The name on her jacket read *Olivia*.

"3320," they said in unison.

"Second car from the back. They're the sleepers." Her smile was inviting and felt like a greeting for more than a train ride. "You headed to a Solstice celebration?" she asked.

Violet's smile grew. "We are. Not our first celebration but it's our first time bringing the Yule log."

Olivia leaned in for a closer look through the plastic wrap. "It looks like a nice one." Her eyes widened when she noticed the roller derby team sticker but she didn't mention it.

"Thank you." Violet tapped the tote with the tip of her shoe. "My aunt usually puts the entire celebration together but this year it's our turn."

"That's amazing. Traditions like that always feel like family to me."

"They really do." Violet pivoted toward the rear of the train. "You celebrate the same way?"

"All my life." Olivia smiled as she stepped away to help another passenger.

"Happy Solstice." As they made their way to the back of the train, Alice internally celebrated the shared holiday greeting. The wheels of the cart thumped against the bubbled safety markings on the platform's surface.

"That was nice." Violet said, affirming Alice's thoughts.

"It was. You never know when you'll get a Solstice greeting."

"It's kinda wonderful to not be erased." As if on queue, Marcus was at the doorway of car 3320.

"Good evening. How are we today?"

"We are excellent," Violet said in a peppy tone, realizing that riding the train might not be as bad as they'd thought.

"That's great to hear. Are the two of you in a sleeper?" he asked.

"We are." Alice lit the screen of her phone.

"That's perfect. You've got the last one in this car." He pointed at the doorway. "Go on in and we'll get your bags checked."

Violet helped Alice lift the tote up and the three of them stood near the luggage room. The storage area wasn't much more than a closet with neatly stacked shelves but Violet was amused by the electric sliding door.

"We'll keep the small bags and just check the tote," Alice said.

"Bag tag for sleeper C." Marcus handed Alice the ticket along with a dining car invitation. "Dinner is served for the next hour. Right up the stairs, take a left and go through the doorway. Wait in the entrance and someone will seat you."

"That's amazing," Violet said.

Alice grinned as she held a hand to her wife. "I'm ready for a meal and an ice-cold beer with my lady. Right after we stow the bags."

"You're the last door to the right," Marcus said, pointing with the notepad in his palm. "Welcome aboard."

All of the sleeper doors were closed as they passed through the cabin and Violet couldn't stop herself from reading the letters as they proceeded, "H, G, F, E & D." She stopped in front of their door. "Ready for our first train cabin?"

"Slide the door, woman, and let's go eat."

The roomette was exactly that. Two seats faced one another with a collapsible table anchored to the wall. Above them was a bunk hinged to the ceiling with white sheets and a blue blanket tucked in around the edges.

"Cozy," Violet said. "Cuddling might be a challenge in here."

"Secluded and so quiet we could make it romantic." Alice slid their door and drew the privacy curtain. "What's the train equivalent of the mile-high club?" She pulled their bodies together.

Violet kissed her. "I have no idea, but I'm game if you are." Her fingers flicked the top buttons of Alice's shirt.

"Romantic dinner first?"

"Are you trying to woo me with fine dining?" She popped another button.

Alice relaxed against their door. "Hell yes I am."

"Dinner and then we come back here and try to figure out how to have dessert in this little roomette."

Alice left the shirt unbuttoned. "Have I told you how much I love you?"

"Every day for the last twenty years." Violet fastened her shirt just enough to cover her wife's sporty bra.

"Good, now let's take advantage of that dining car."

# CHAPTER TWELVE

The dining car on the train had booth-style benches on both sides. There were enough to seat more than eighty people, which was not quite as intimate as either of the women had anticipated.

"Welcome to the dining car." The attendant was tall—almost too tall for the height clearance of the train car. Her dark-blue uniform, although synthetic, had a form-fitting cut that suited the woman's curvy figure. "My name is Bethany and I'll be taking care of you. Do you have a dining ticket?"

Alice gave her the reservation slip from Marcus.

"Perfect. Follow me, please."

Alice noticed the children occupying three of the booth spaces ahead of them. "Is it possible to sit in the quiet booth in the corner?" She pointed to the opposite end of the train car.

"Oh, no. That's for staff breaks." Bethany paused in front of a booth already occupied by a couple. "Please have a seat." She waved at the benches.

Disappointed to sit with strangers, they took their place near the center of the car. Each table around them was filled with what appeared to be the largest family on the planet with the worst-behaving children Alice would never wish for.

"Kinda loud for dinner," Violet whispered.

The man beside her said, "They're our great-grandchildren. They can get kinda squirmy this time of day."

"Oh great." Alice smirked. "So this is your family?"

The woman beside her smiled. "All of us, yes. I'm Earnestine and this is my husband, Bertram."

Violet raised an amused eyebrow to her wife.

"Nice to meet you," Alice said. "I'm Alice, and this is my wife Violet."

"Lovely to meet you, and the rest of the people in here make up four generations of Willoughbys."

"Four, that's pretty amazing." Alice felt the thump of a child's foot hitting the back of her bench seat."

"That's my truck." The tallest of the children grabbed the metal car.

"Fuck!" the little one in blue screamed.

"It's 'truck', Penny," he corrected, tucking the little monster truck behind his back.

"Fuck!" she yelled louder this time and her great-grandfather reached to take the palm-sized monster truck from the boy.

"Let's let Penny play with it for a little while." His voice was scolding but the boy respected the decision and crawled under the table to play with the three bulldozers beneath it.

"My apologies. Little Penny just started to talk and can't quite make the *TR* sound." Earnestine fought to hide her amusement.

"It's adorable to hear that word with a pixie's voice," Alice said, amused.

"But that boy." Bertram tsked. "I think he understands exactly what she's saying and instigates just to hear her yell it."

"It's a different generation, Bertram," Violet said.

"It certainly is."

Alice felt the child at her hip, attempting to climb across and sit in her great-grandmother's lap.

"Would you mind?" Earnestine asked.

Alice stood and the little girl crawled on the seat.

Violet laughed at the situation of this tiny, foul-mouthed human cuddled beside her wife. Alice did not like children—especially squirmy ones that screamed obscenities while she was trying to have a romantic meal.

"Oh, that won't do for dinner," Bethany said, noticing the lack of elbow room. "I shouldn't do this but can I ask you to move to the bench behind here so they have more space?"

Although a little put off by the lack of concern for their comfort as a couple, Alice was delighted to move away from the wild group overtaking the dinner car.

Violet popped up. "We'd love to give the children more time with their great-grandparents."

Alice and Violet slid into the booth behind them, enjoying the side-by-side seating.

"What can I get the two of you to drink?" Bethany asked, setting the paper menus in front of them. "This is tonight's dinner menu but I'll warn you we are out of the Sirloin steak and the grilled chicken."

"I'll have a glass of red wine if you have it."

"Scotch, neat please." Alice's head fell against the seat.

"I'll be right back."

"Scotch, huh?" Violet's hand slid to her wife's thigh.

"Maybe it will erase the memory of a toddler yelling the F-word on a train."

"Probably not," Violet said, laughing. She picked up the paper menu, browsing the dinner options, and flipped it over to look for more. "Well, this is fun," she said as she raised the blank backside of the menu. "We can have cheese pizza or we can have cheese pizza with pepperoni."

"You're kidding me."

Bethany returned with their drinks. "Have we decided on a dinner option?" She placed the glasses in front of them.

"The fish option is crossed out, so the only option is pizza?" Alice asked. The last thing she wanted at nearly eight at night was a heavy gut-load of pizza dough.

"I'm so sorry. We didn't receive our fish at the four o'clock stop so it wasn't even on the dinner menu tonight. Yes, pizza is the only option, or I could make you a salad?"

"Salad and scotch sounds like a perfectly romantic dinner pairing." Alice took a sip of her drink, swallowing hard on the absolute bottom-shelf flavor tingling in her mouth.

Bethany picked up on her displeasure. "Not good?"

"Oh, it's the worst. I absolutely hate Johnnie Walker."

"A real scotch drinker." Bethany nodded with approval.

"If my girl knows anything, she knows how to tie a woman in and the sipping quality of single-malt scotch." Violet squeezed her wife's hand.

"Can I get you something else?" Bethany asked.

"Since I'm having salad for dinner, how about a glass of whatever you poured for my wife?"

"Absolutely. And will you be ordering a salad, also, or the pizza?"

Violet smiled. "I'll have the pepperoni pizza."

"Perfect. I'll put that in and bring you a glass of wine."

Alice's shoulders tensed at the sound of a baby fussing. Violet squeezed her wife's hand.

"Of course there's a baby."

There wasn't enough wine on the train to take the edge off their dining experience. Ten minutes of Willoughby train car occupation was almost too much.

"Do you think we can take the food to our roomette?" Alice asked.

"Pizza and salad in that little closet?" Violet said. "I think we can survive right here. You've pushed through worse."

"Oh sure, make me the villain in this scenario."

Before Violet could respond, the food arrived at their table. The pizza was little more than fast food but the salad was impressively dressed with fresh vegetables and a sliced hard-boiled egg.

"Can I get you anything else?" Bethany asked just before Penny screeched her enthusiastic demand for the metal truck.

"Noise-canceling headphones for two?" Alice mumbled but it was loud enough for the attendant to hear.

"Oh, trust me, if I had some, I'd be wearing them myself."

The laughs that followed settled Alice enough to stay in their seats. The rest of their meal continued about the same. The Willoughby family remained a rowdy bunch. Violet and Alice forced down their dinner and didn't waste time as they backtracked through the dining car to return to their roomette.

"I am so glad we never had children." Alice snickered as they exited the dining car. Their dinner, from start to finish, had been as far from romantic as it could get.

"The little curly-headed one was cute." Vi's attempt to salvage their evening was not going to work.

"That one was new."

"Oh love, new?" Violet teased.

"No! You have to give that to me, Vi. The kid wasn't terrible because all they do at that age is eat, sleep and shit, and not necessarily in that order." She was animated as they walked down the narrow corridor past the larger family-sized rooms.

"Coffee?" Alice stopped to fill a cup.

"Too late for me and I'm liking the way the wine took the edge off this catastrophe of an evening."

Alice dispensed a half cup before giving it a little sip. "You sure? It's kinda good."

"I love you but there isn't a cup of coffee or anything on this planet that's going to make me want to be awake any longer than necessary right now."

Alice balanced the cup in her splinted hand so she could hold Violet's. "This trip has to be the worst in a very long time."

Violet squeezed their tangled fingers, making a statement with the gesture that Alice understood. Once upon a time they'd had a terrible trip. In actuality, it was their first trip together as adrenaline junkies, and it would always be their worst experience.

"I fell in love with you on that *worst trip ever*," Alice whispered.

"You saved me in more ways than one." Violet turned to ascend the stairs leading to their sleeper roomette.

"We were lucky that day." Alice waited as her wife opened their door. She knew another conversation was coming; it almost always happened when Alice reached her emotional limits. What she needed right now was a sit down with her therapist.

Violet relaxed, pushing the suitcase against her legs so Alice could sit across from her. "Baby, we weren't lucky. You and Britt and Stacey knew what you were doing and we are all alive because of it."

"Yeah, there was some luck involved, too."

"Greta was the lucky one."

Alice chuckled. "Who knew a venomous snakebite could actually save a life?" The statement was sarcastic but also true.

Violet shoved the suitcase against the doorway of their room. "There are always risks involved when you take nature on. You planned for animal attacks and, without that plan, Britt wouldn't be working in the park because she wouldn't be alive."

"I know."

"Come over here." She snaked a finger to summon her stubborn lover. "I think you might need to be a little spoon."

"Darlin', I don't think either of us gets to be a spoon in this cardboard-box-sized compartment tonight."

The foot pedal and slide mechanisms that converted their single chairs into something a little bigger than a toddler bed required an engineering degree to engage. Fortunately, between the two of them, they were amply equipped.

Alice pointed to the upper bunk, trying her best to avoid the serious direction the conversation had taken. "I could top you tonight."

Violet shook her head, smiling. "Not tonight." She pulled the pillows from the bunk above them. "Lay here with me."

"This isn't big enough."

"We'll fit. Come here."

Alice, as she almost always did, acquiesced to the only person she trusted enough to protect her. She knew what those arms would do when they wrapped around her. "Vi, I love you, you know."

"I do know, and that's why I'm here."

"I really don't want to talk about the cougar anymore," Alice whispered.

"You never do and then suddenly you do." Violet rumpled under the hem of her wife's shirt, laying her palm flat against the solid carved muscles of her stomach. Her fingertip caressed the scar on Alice's hip, pausing for a long moment to remember the hooked flesh where the animal fought and clawed to get a deeper hold on Brittney's hand. The animal met one barrier that sunny day; it had to get through Alice. Not one member of their team made it out of the national park unscarred.

"I miss those days."

"I miss some of them," Vi whispered.

"Yeah."

~~~~~~~~~~

"Why?" Alice pushed off the bed. There wasn't enough space to turn away from the screeching coming from outside their roomette. There wasn't an extra pillow to cover her ears or enough power in noise-canceling headphones to block the sound out, even if she had a pair.

"Five! One tr…uck, two tr…uck!" The child's voice faded.

"I think every Willoughby child from dinner is in this car with us."

Violet tried not to laugh, and failed, which only made her wife grumpier.

Alice pushed the curtain to peek into the narrow space that was their hallway. "One, two and there's a third kid, and the hallway is scattered with toy cars at—" she looked at her watch—"eleven fifteen." She let the curtain fall. "They are letting their three smallest children run up and down like they
~~~~~~~~~~

own the whole train when the little noseminers should be sleeping."

"Come and lay back down. There's nothing we can do."

"Love, I can't lay down, and you know it." Alice flipped the lock's secondary latch and slid the door wide enough to pop her head out. The door at the end of the hallway behind her was closed. Hopefully whoever was inside had brought a set of noise-canceling headphones with them. "Hello." Her whisper was loud enough to stop the children where they stood.

"Mommy!" the smallest one squealed.

In response, a curtain slid open just before a head peeked through. "Please, just play. You don't need any more cars to fight over."

"Excuse me, hi." Alice waved with her splinted wrist. "Trying to get some sleep down here."

The woman froze, her eyes wide. "Oh, shit."

Alice nodded.

"I didn't know anyone was in that room." Her hand came up to cover her face as a flush of red rimmed her throat, traveling up to what Alice could see of her face.

"No shit, really." A man's bearded face peeked out and Alice wanted to pop each one of them like a whack-a-mole.

"Yes, really, and we've had a day, and would honestly like to sleep."

"Donnie, Bobbie, Rickie…" He called the children and it wasn't a surprise that none of them responded.

"Boys!" The woman said the single word with teeth clenched and lips tight.

Alice chortled when all the dark, curly heads poked out from the bottom of the stairs. "Get over here."

Violet popped her head out to see the lineup. She felt horrible that the children were being scolded for doing what children did when there were no limits.

Violet and Alice couldn't hear the mother as she whispered instructions and the children disappeared into the row of roomettes.

"They'll behave now." Her tone held certainty that neither Alice nor Violet trusted as they leaned back into their tiny slice of the train-car pie.

"Was that all of the kids at dinner tonight?" Violet unbuttoned her shirt and hung it from the slender cabinet hook.

"It sounded like twice as many, but I'm not a great judge." Alice wrapped herself around her wife. "I'm so glad we didn't do that."

Violet's sigh was loud. "Me too, but I think we could have done it better than that."

"Maybe." There was no regret in Alice's voice, no longing for a rewind of time that would accommodate children, at all.

They crawled into what was an extremely tight single bed, doing their best to snuggle in for the rest of the ride. The promise of quiet children lasted less than thirty minutes. Violet and Alice surrendered to what was left of their nightmare ride.

~~~~~~~~~~

The knocking woke Violet first and she was quick to straddle her wife and hold her in place. "I'll get it."

"I've never understood murder on a train as much as I do right now." Alice's voice was sleep blurred and husky, a tone
~~~~~~~~~~

that fell into position number two on Violet's top ten list of Alice sounds.

"Stay right here." Violet pushed her wife against the bed with one finger tip.

Alice's hands came up to hold her thighs. "You should stay right here and join the mile post club with me."

There was more knocking, but Violet was intrigued. "Mile post, what now?"

"I searched the web. It's the equivalent of the mile high club for flying but it's mile post when someone is fucking on a train."

Vi shook her finger. "So naughty."

Alice's smile grew and she wiggled her eyebrows. "Your position is just about—"

The knock was loud, followed by a voice neither expected. "There's one stop before you disembark."

"Marcus," they said together. Violet arched away from her wife, banging her head on the upper bunk.

"Ouch!" she yelled.

A muffled voice asked, "Everything alright?"

Violet rubbed her head. "Just fine, thank you. We'll be ready."

"We could go for the meter post club." Alice thrust her pelvis and if Vi wasn't still rubbing her head she would have clunked it again.

"You're so bad."

"I can also be very good." Alice sat forward, her hand holding tight to her wife's ass.

"Uh huh, I have experience—" The position shift caused Violet to grab hold of Alice's shoulders and before she could take a breath she was facing the opposite direction with a very amorous woman nibbling her collarbone. Their bodies lurched as the train's speed reduced by half. "One stop and we have to go." Violet's voice was breathy.

"Challenge—"

"Luggage will be pulled in fifteen minutes." The voice spoke through the door again.

"I can do you in five."

The button popped on Violet's pants and just before Alice's fingers dipped inside, Violet found her wits. "We are not fucking on this train right now." She grabbed the roaming hand.

"You sure?" Alice tickled her skin.

"Woman!"

Alice couldn't hold her wife with her splinted wrist. "One false move and your ass is gonna hit the floor."

Violet knelt hard against the makeshift bed, grabbed the bunk above her and stretched to stand. This new position gave Alice the perfect opportunity to grab hold and place a long, hard kiss against the exposed soft skin of her wife's belly.

"Oh fuck, love. That's not going to get us off this train."

"At the moment, getting you off is my only—."

Violet pushed away, adjusting the half-cocked shirt on her shoulder with a circular arm swing. "You're such an…"

"Adoring wife?"

"At the very least, but there isn't time for what we were about to do."

Alice flopped back, banging her head on the collapsible table. "Ow!" She raised her splinted hand to rub the spot she bumped. "Perfect, just perfect."

Vi tugged Alice's good hand. "Don't be so foolish. Kiss me and we'll take care of each other when strangers aren't banging on our door."

Alice raised an eyebrow, questioning whether both of them could find the alone time at Aunt Eunice's house. "I don't believe you."

Violet spun her wife into the doorway, pinning her against the wall and the suitcase at their knees. She hit the pedal on the floor and the bed transformed into two seats, and she pushed her wife into one of them.

Vi winked, "Wait and see, hot stuff."

There wasn't time to grab hold of Violet and drag her back. She was already flipping the security latch and tugging the sliding door open. The hallway was quiet at nearly three a.m. The curtain climbers must have finally collapsed, emptied of the sugar rush.

"The coast is clear." Violet grabbed her wife's hand. "Let's escape while we can."

An announcement for the next stop came over the speaker system and they felt the momentum of the train shift to slower speed. Alice carried the duffle like a cross-shoulder sling bag, dragging her wife's suitcase behind them.

# CHAPTER THIRTEEN

"Your bags." Marcus stepped over the gap between the train car and the station platform to set their Yule log tote attached to the wheeled cart on the dimpled surface.

"Thank you, Marcus." Alice held out her hand, discreetly passing him a twenty dollar tip.

"You all travel safely," he said, shoving his hand into his pocket.

"We'll do our best." Violet smiled. "Happy holidays."

"Same to you and yours." He waved twice and secured the door behind him.

The station stop lasted long enough for people to get off and on. Before they could say another word, the wheels squealed into motion and they waited for the train to pull away before approaching the station.

"Is it terrible that I want to be at home right now?" Alice whispered as they crossed the concrete platform of the train station. From the echo of their surroundings it felt like she and Violet were the only passengers who'd exited the train, and Alice had no idea why she was whispering.

"It's been a long few days." Violet blew out a cleansing breath. "And I confess I'd like to be in our bed right now."

"Three a.m. is too damn early after the day we had," Alice said.

"But we made it," Violet said, being the ray of sunshine that she was.

"We did, but poor Eunice," Alice said. "Maybe we should have hired a taxi to take us to her house."

"I felt terrible when I called her. I don't think she heard half of the story about our trip but she promised she'd be here to get us."

"Your aunt is such a trooper." Alice used a foot to help her wife lift the tote over the revolving mechanism of the escalator stairs.

"I'll bet you she's right outside the exit, open arms and all."

"That's a sucker's bet," Alice said, as they topped the staircase. The escalator let off a few feet from the inner doors of the station and there was one public safety officer patrolling the empty space.

Violet's guess couldn't have been more accurate as the glass doors opened and they walked out to waiting arms.

Eunice looked a little smaller than she'd been in October. Her silver hair was twisted in a braid that hung down her back. The smock she wore was slightly better than a housecoat and it was the absolute minimum required to pick up train ride passengers. Alice eyed the boots on the woman's feet—perhaps the quirkiest combination of rubber and athletic shoe. Eunice definitely had a style all of her own.

"A most blessed Yule to you, my darlings." Eunice's voice was oddly alert at the early hour as she stood on shaky legs to greet them exactly as predicted.

Violet was humbled by the enthusiasm, again worried about bothering her aunt to pick them up in the dark, but she'd insisted and here they were standing in the mild night air of a very quiet train station.

Eunice hugged Violet before turning to Alice who was tangled in luggage. A shaky, arthritic, hard-working hand patted Alice's cheek. "And the happiest of Yule to you, darling Alice."

"Thank you, Eunice." Alice's arms raised for a hug.

Eunice cradled the splinted wrist. "It appears you've had an adventure."

"You don't even know the half of it." Alice smiled, not wanting to share the ridiculous details of their last two days.

As they approached the car, she was struck by the ridiculousness of the vehicle's size. This mid-eighties gas guzzler was almost capable of carrying the Fiat 500 and the yellow Yaris that rescued them after Bess's crash.

With shaky hands, Eunice put the key in to unlock the back door. "Everything will have to go inside with us. The trunk is full of decorations and some surprises for the celebration." She pushed the unlock button for the other doors.

Alice maneuvered the Yule log tote to fit in the front seat at an odd angle and wedged their bags behind it, taking up a third of the back seat. The drive was cozy and Alice took every opportunity to remind Violet that she was still eager to make that mile high, or mile post, club.

"So how's old Bess doing?" Eunice pumped the gas pedal with the vigor of a fifteen-year-old student driver and turned the key. The engine didn't purr; it made a sound that reminded Violet and Alice of their borrowed red Fiat. They looked at each other and their unspoken worry faded as the engine revved a little more than it should.

"Last text message we got was that Bess had a shiny new windshield and was getting some fresh paint," Violet explained.

"Terrible thing."

"It could have been worse," Alice interrupted, making sure her wife knew that she was already letting go of blame for their mishap.

"Yes, yes. No one was hurt and that's most important." Aunt Eunice had a no-nonsense way about her, simple in almost every manner. "Your celebratory creation looks pretty spiffy in there." She knocked her knuckles against the tote, proving that she might be slower but wasn't fragile or frail. "You've got it shut up in that box—very good job."

Alice smiled, waiting for the teasing to begin.

"That thing's had quite an adventure," Violet explained. "I'm not sure what we would have done if it wasn't in that container."

"The wheeled cart is a nice touch." Eunice tapped the metal frame that was still attached to the tote. Her car had manual transmission and her grinding of the gears as she shifted into reverse made both rear passengers tense.

"We picked the cart up from the roller derby team," Alice said. She knew what was coming next and couldn't wait to hear her wife explain the team name.

Eunice looked at the couple in the mirror. "Those are the Whores if I remember correctly, yes?" she asked without a shift in expression. The clutch popped, jerking their heads against the forward motion.

"The Whore Moans, yes, Auntie, and Stacey says hello and sends lots of hugs to you."

"She's a lovely girl, that one." Eunice pulled into traffic and Violet felt the death grip of her wife's hand. Alice never liked being a passenger and she most definitely didn't enjoy riding in the back seat.

"She sent a gift for you, too," Vi told her.

"Oh, how lovely."

Alice snickered. "You're absolutely going to love it."

# CHAPTER FOURTEEN

With the skill of a NASCAR driver, Eunice backed her tank of a car into the detached garage, turned off the engine and laid the keys on the dashboard. "Take the car if you need it. Keys are always right here." She patted the ring.

"Thank you, Auntie," Violet said, "but I don't think we are getting into a car until it's time to go home." She looked at her wife for confirmation. Alice closed her eyes and gave a deep-affirming nod.

"Either way, you know what to do. The coffee is set to brew in the morning—" Eunice looked at her watch—"which is only a few hours off, so make yourself at home."

"We will," Alice said. "And thanks again for picking us up."

"It was my pleasure." The hinge of the driver's door squeaked as Eunice opened it. "You're upstairs, as always. Room's all set up just for you and we can leave the Yule log here for now." She patted the plastic container. "I'm going to rest for a little while; maybe you want to take a nap, too?"

"Wake us if you need help, and yes, I think your suggestion of a nap will hit the spot," Vi said, smiling as she paused to appreciate the unnatural glow of the landscape rocks along the pathway to the house. "These are very festive." She crouched to touch the glowing stones.

"Aren't they glorious? They were a gift and I just love the way they light up the path."

"Fun and functional," Violet quipped. Alice offered a hand to help her wife stand.

"Who knew glowing rocks could make someone so happy?" Eunice asked, opening the door.

"We're shooting for small victories at the moment," Alice said as they followed Eunice into the house.

The kitchen was aglow from a stained-glass nightlight near the coffee maker. The colors danced across the ceiling, adding to the festive greeting from the sidewalk stones. As they walked through the house, the decorations of evergreen sprigs and the scent of fresh-cut pine flooded their senses. This was what Solstice was meant to feel like. Alice let out a sigh of relief at reaching their destination.

"See you in a little while," Eunice said as she disappeared into her bedroom.

"See you in a bit," Vi replied.

On weary legs, Violet and Alice climbed to the second story. It wasn't a surprise that the spare bedroom was draped in rainbows with every bit of pride swag an ally could collect after a lifetime of supporting the queer community. The bedspread design had hand-sized arching rainbows with the phrase 'love is love' printed beneath each. Maybe a little juvenile, but it was almost like getting a giant hug from Eunice. The walls held gorgeous popsicle-stick-framed artwork made by Eunice's summer school children for the library art show. Every inch of the space dripped with love. Violet had always been safe in this house and her aunt was the reason.

"This room is kinda gay." Alice wrapped her arms around her wife from behind.

"Gayer now that you're here." Violet relaxed into the embrace.

"The absolute gayest with the two of us." She chuckled.

"That woman has always been ahead of her time and I don't know what I would have done without her." Vi's head fell back against her wife's shoulder.

"You know, she said we should take a nap." Alice rotated her wrist to display her watch face. "How about we get under that very gay comforter and snuggle?"

Violet pointed at the unicorn pillow. "We aren't having sex in that gay bed. At least, not right now." She winked at her wife.

Alice began slow-walking them across the room. "But baby, love is love."

Violet felt a vibration coming from her wife's pocket. "Ooh, nice timing."

Alice chuckled. "That's probably the confirmation of our next phase of this trip from hell."

"Is it your boyfriend?" Violet wriggled tighter against her wife, preventing her from extracting her phone.

"It might be. Let me look, woman." Alice's phone continued to buzz as she read the screen. "It's my boyfriend and he says yes and that he loves you and will see us soon." She tossed the phone on her duffle bag.

"He'll get us to Bess?" Violet reached behind her back to unfasten her bra. She threaded it through her sleeve and tossed it at her wife.

"He will definitely get us to Bess." Alice snatched the undergarment out of the air. With two long strides, her hands were on Violet and they toppled onto the bed.

~~~~~~~~~~
~~~~~~~~~~

"What is that noise?" Alice asked through throaty mumbles.

"A bee caught in a fiddle?" Violet grunted, and buried her head against her wife's shoulder.

"Uh uh," Alice groaned.

"Bagpipes?" Violet thought she was dreaming, hardly conscious of anything but the odd sound coming through the corner speaker.

"No, I don't think it could be, unless there are electric bagpipes?"

"Is that a thing?" Violet rolled tighter into her wife's arms.

"If not, I don't have a clue."

Violet whimpered. "Do you think she realizes the speakers are on in here?"

"Not one single bit." Alice rubbed the small of her wife's back, making slow circles. "Should we get up?"

"We probably should since whatever that noise is, it's not a lullaby."

They were slow to move in the dark as they dressed, careful not to disturb the atmosphere Eunice had set. In any other house, the sound coming from the speakers would vibrate with jingling bells and ho ho ho-ing, but not Eunice's. She had her mysterious instrument plinking through the sound system in the house. It was quirky and oddly satisfying, like a naked winter snowstorm frolic, but the occasional shrill was grossly irritating and the balancing imbalance was everything you'd expect during a celebration in this house.

As they opened the bedroom door, the aroma of spiced wine filled the hallway. "I think I love your aunt almost as much as I love her spiced wine," Alice whispered.

"She can definitely summon the Pagans with the concoction she's got brewing in the kitchen," Violet replied.

"I'm hooked."

"Stop lingering in the hallway and get your butts down here." Eunice's voice was loud, almost scolding if you didn't know her ways. She was holding the remote for the device she called her music maker up over her head, waving it like a wand to reduce the volume of the instrumental track playing.

Alice laughed as she approached, reaching for the woman's wrist to redirect it toward the sound system mounted in the dining-room cabinet. "Your music maker is right over there."

"Yes, yes, I know, but the battery is getting low and I find that if I wave it like this it eventually makes a connection." Eunice continued waving her remote and flailed like a band conductor on their podium.

"You're amazing, Auntie." Violet stepped in to hug her and passed the remote to her wife. "Batteries are in the zipper pocket in my suitcase."

"Got it." Alice turned around, noticing the case for the CD that was playing. "Hurdy-gurdy!" she yelled, identifying the instrument as she walked away.

"It's terrifying," Violet yelled in response. Her Aunt waved off their lack of enthusiasm for the music.

The remote control battery exchange was a predictable part of their seasonal visits, switching them out and updating the technology that Eunice couldn't be bothered learning but enjoyed using. Alice stepped into the study, smiling as she appreciated the turntable with a pair of over-the-ear headphones with a spiraling cord attached. Even with the whole-house sound system Alice installed years ago, Aunt Eunice wasn't giving up her long playing albums.

Alice switched the batteries in the remote, and then reached inside the record cabinet and checked the needle on the record player. "All systems go," she whispered to herself as she followed the laughter coming from the kitchen.

"Climbing is all legs and hips," Eunice said, gyrating and twisting as she pointed her spoon toward Alice. The seventy year old's bouldering dance was only adorable because she was doing it to tease Alice.

Alice held her hands up in surrender. "I know, I know."

"At least you didn't break it." Eunice repeated Violet's words, agreeing with the assessment made on the way out of the urgent-care facility.

"You and my wife need to stop colluding."

"I think we will keep reminding you that risks, for risk's sake, are always risky," Eunice said and Violet laughed.

Alice shook her head as she swooped around the kitchen island to take a peek at the pot simmering on the cooktop. "What's my favorite crone cooking up for the Solstice celebration?"

"All the little lads left over from the Samhain celebration." Eunice's laugh echoed against the lid of the pot as she raised it.

"You have to stop calling your herbs little lads." Alice took a deep breath. "Oh, that smells wonderful."

"Mulled wine and spiced bread is in the oven for our guests tonight."

Violet reached for her wife's wrist, rotating it to check her watch. "Do we have a little time to set the fire pit?"

"You can have all the time you want before the sun sets."

"Can you join us?" Alice inched toward the front door. "We promise to help with the rest of the prep."

"I suppose the bread will bake and the pot doesn't need much watching." She turned the burner down on the cooktop and set the timer on the oven. "There's not much left to do in the ring. Since I didn't need to hunt for the log this year, I had plenty of time to make it festive."

"It's always festive, Auntie, and we are so ready to turn the Wheel and enjoy the sun's rebirth."

"Ahh, longer daylight means more mischief." Alice held her bent arm to Eunice and they walked out together into the yard. The sun was low in the sky and it was clear that although the evening would be intimate, with only six chairs around the circle, it was bound to be a hearty celebration.

"You're making an awful lot of wine for tonight." Violet waved at the chairs set in a circle.

"I'm expecting more people this year. I just wanted to make sure anyone who needs it has a place to rest." She tapped her cane against the fire pit stones. "Some of us need to take a break once in a while."

"I'll be right here all night if you need me," Alice offered and held the back of the chair while Eunice sat down.

"Why don't you drag that container out here and let's have a look at what you brought for us."

Alice walked away, leaving Eunice and Violet alone. "Thank you again for picking us up this morning."

"Oh dear, I'm hardly ever asleep these days. It's the joy of retirement that I can take my little naps whenever I want." She chuckled. "It was my pleasure to pick you up."

Violet adjusted the stones of their fire ring, pushing a gap between a few to allow air to feed tonight's fire. She squatted beside the weathered tin pail, fluffing bundles of tinder. "We're glad we made it in time to turn the Wheel with you."

"It wouldn't be much of a celebration without my Violet and Alice."

Violet turned at the squealing thump, thump, thumping of the Yule log cart against the patio paver bricks.

"Here we go. For better or worse." Alice released the bungee hooks and placed the tote on the ground in front of Eunice. The woman chuckled as Alice cut away the plastic wrapping, making a cautious slice around the Whore Moans sticker.

The crinkling plastic and the clicking release of the container's lid were not the most elegant way to present the Yule log, but Alice and Violet were still excited. They knew every tiny detail about the contents but the anticipation of Eunice's reaction was almost too much to bear.

"The oils are the perfect blend." Eunice scooped the air, pulling the scent toward her heart. "The aroma is very nice." She removed the bundle of candles, holding one end of the wrapping as it twirled in her lap. "Your candle choices are excellent." She handed them to her niece.

"That was all Violet," Alice's voice was soft. "She picked them from the batch you made for us last year."

"Given, not bought. Very good." Eunice bent in an awkward position to lift the festive bundle of aspen limbs from the tote.

"Let me help you." Alice reached over at the same time Violet reached in and they bumped heads. It was the final straw for Alice. "Ow! Really, universe?" she yelled at the sky. "I feel like our Yule log is somehow cursing this celebration." She rubbed her head as she plopped to sit on the fire circle stones.

Violet rubbed her forehead as she watched her aunt lift their treasure from the travel container and slow-walk it to the fire circle.

"There is no curse, only what is meant to be and the power of love that traveled from your back yard to mine." Eunice closed her eyes, placing her palm against the Aspen bundle. "You have most soulfully presented the spirit of Solstice," she whispered.

"Thank you, Auntie. We did everything we could to make it perfect for you."

For the first time, Alice surveyed the fire circle Eunice used to celebrate the turning of the Wheel. Imbolc's February turning of the Wheel was always Alice's favorite celebration because Eunice made the best honey and seed cakes.

Tonight, the Yule celebration of light was the focus. The very first time she and Vi had come for Yule, almost twenty years earlier, Alice was in awe that the shortest day of sunlight was the actual celebration of the return to longer days. During that celebration, which held Alice's heart, she had understood—for the first time, with certainty—what a spiritual home felt like.

"The ring is already cleared?" Alice asked, and Eunice smiled as she placed the Yule log in the center of their burn circle. The stones surrounding it had a history of their own—each one found on an adventure in some magical space. River rocks and farm fieldstones, stacked together, made Eunice's backyard the perfect place to turn the Wheel of the Year.

"If I don't clear the ring, we can't harvest the ash for Imbolc."

"I know that, but I usually clear the ring for you after Samhain. It's tradi—."

Eunice held up one finger, silencing Alice. “You brought the Yule log, my darlings. The new tradition means we will all change the way we participate.”

“So mote it be,” Violet said with a smile.

Eunice smiled. “So mote it be. Now head off and write your letters for the lighting ceremony.”

Violet dragged Alice away from the circle and into the house where Eunice had a station of supplies waiting.

“What’s your wish for the year?” Alice asked.

“For one more year with you.” Violet pecked her wife on the cheek.

Alice sat at the table, selecting a light-green note card for her message. “You write that every year.”

“And so far my wish has come true.”

# CHAPTER FIFTEEN

"I can't believe I was wearing your bra." Alice adjusted the undergarment before pulling her shirt over it.

"It felt different, but whatever." Violet waved off the exchange. "Your bra, my bra—either way, it's getting the job done."

"You're so easy." Alice switched off the bedroom light and they made their way through the house.

"I'm only easy for you," Violet whispered as she bumped into her wife's backside.

"It's kinda dark, don't trip." Alice held out her splinted hand to guide Violet from the back door through the yard. She could smell the fresh scent of cranberry and orange from the garlands Eunice had tied among the tree limbs. The edible gifts were for all the wild creatures as they endured the winter season.

"Darlin', it's dark on purpose." Violet paused, tugging their bodies together.

"Uh huh, and I always look forward to the pre-lighting part of the celebration, because I can do this." Alice pressed her lips against Violet's, and in the moment they felt anchored to each other and the season.

"Feeling better, now that we're here?" Violet asked.

Alice's forehead rested against her wife's. "Eunice has an amazing way of creating space that takes me away from the outside world."

Their arms tightened around each other. "She really does," Vi agreed.

"Hello, my lovely dears." Aunt Eunice's arms came around them and they shared a quick huddling group hug. The woman was bathed in the scent of the season, with sage and rosemary lingering in the air.

"Auntie, we were just enjoying the circle you've created."

"Very good things happen in the dark." It was impossible to know for sure but Alice was certain a mischievous grin followed as her aunt tapped her cane-style staff against the stones of the gathering place. "Come on, let's celebrate the coming of the light."

Alice and Violet recognized many of the people in Eunice's circle of friends, with the exception of a silver-haired androgynous person standing behind Eunice's place on the circle.

"Hello, my dear." Eunice patted the person's face, their eyes meeting before a kiss that touched each cheek.

"I'm excited to be here," they said with a smile.

"Come and meet my beauties." She held a hand to Violet. "My niece, practically daughter, Violet, and her wife Alice." She brought them closer together. "This is Simone. My new friend."

"Hello." Alice held out her hand, and the greeting was a mutual sizing-up of two strong individuals.

"Friend?" Violet wasn't shy to ask.

"Yes, they've been a delightful addition to my life."

"Eunice and I do art together," Simone explained.

"Really?" Alice questioned.

"I direct all of the summer youth programs," Simone added.

"Hmm." The throaty noise Alice made was hardly a response and Violet could sense her wife's fiercely protective nature awakening.

"Calm down, burly one," Violet whispered.

"Maybe I will, but not yet," she said as the hurdy-gurdy plinked and the drumming circle initiated the evening's celebration.

"Gather here, you all, and Blessed be," Eunice sing-songed as she sparked a flame to the candle on the pedestal in front of her. "Tonight is the feast and our celebration of light. Did you all write your wish letters?"

Many hands in the circle waved with folded pieces of paper inside.

"Wonderful." The musicians played behind her as Simone moved the candle onto the stone ring.

Eunice disappeared into the shadows and returned with a basket twice the size of her hands. "As the vessel moves around the circle, choose a pinecone and tuck your wish letters into the seed scale of it." A few people questioned the instructions as the basket made its way from person to person. "Those are the little parts that look like dragon scales," she explained.

Alice was patient for the basket to come around. The large wicker container required two hands to hold, and each person shared in the selection process. Violet loved the tradition.

"They smell wonderful," one of the women said as the basket moved to her hands.

"Like Winter Solstice," Violet whispered as she held the basket for her wife.

"Just like our kitchen." Alice winked. "Thank you, love."

Simone was the last to carry the half-empty wicker container, placing it beside Eunice's chair.

One by one, each person set their pinecone wish beside the Yule log. With the steadiest hands, Eunice took the celebration candle and touched each of the candles anchored in the bore holes Alice had drilled into the Yule log.

"Tonight, the goddess Lucia is the bringer of light. We say farewell to the long nights and welcome the return of the sun and longer days."

"Blessed be," someone whispered, and the rest of the circle repeated the words.

Eunice touched the cauldron charcoal to her candle flame and a dance of sparkly flares brought the smolder for burning incense.

"Come, my darling, Violet." She waved her niece closer. "Hold out your hand."

Violet opened her palm, cupping it, ready to receive the celebratory resins they would burn.

"Frankincense, ruled by the sun to bring abundance." Eunice placed the pebble of resin in Violet's hand. "Juniper, to remember life and protect us through this new year." She placed the dehydrated berry in Violet's palm.

Eunice continued through her list until Violet had a small collection of herbs and resins in her cupped hands.

Together, Eunice and Violet placed the herbs on the glowing charcoal and the rising smoke wafted through the Solstice circle. The smell was like a dream, and it made Violet believe anything was possible as she felt her wife's arms wrap around her. Nothing could be more magical than the energy moving through the people in this circle.

The music played on for hours. They celebrated each phase of the fire progressing from candle light to bonfire flame as the wish pinecones ignited inside the circle. The celebration of Yule was underway.

~~~~~~~~~~~

"So how will you get Bess back?" Eunice asked.

They sat around the smoldering Yule log. The celebration had gone late into the night and one by one all of her friends returned to their homes, leaving the four of them to enjoy the cool winter air. The night was so dark that constellations disappeared into billions of unnamed shining stars.

Violet's head was resting on Alice's shoulder. She said, "We have to meet up with Britt to get Bess."

"You remember Britt, right?" Alice asked.

The firelight shone on Eunice's face, seriousness reflecting in her eyes. "She's the one who lost her fingers?"

Simone's eyes went wide. The glare of the fire spotlighted her surprised expression.

"An accident on the trail. It was a long time ago." Eunice tapped Simone's knee. "Remember we talked about it?"

"I do. It just… I wasn't expecting…" Simone stopped talking.

Alice's body tensed. "Since you know the story I won't pretend, or downplay, that Britt saved my life at the same time she was fighting for her own."

"It was *you,* your leadership and the trust you built, that saved the entire team, and neither Britt nor Stacey ever lost focus. That's how all of us survived." Violet sat forward, moving closer to the heat of the fire to shake the sudden chill. It didn't matter how many years passed; triggers came from
~~~~~~~~~~~

nowhere, and sometimes they appeared from everywhere, and the animal attack was always going to be part of them.

"Britt is back there. She's a park ranger now and she was there to help us again with Bess, which is kinda wild if you think about it." Alice whispered the last bit mostly to herself.

"The wild part is that your connection is far-reaching and tonight of all nights we send love and energies of healing to our soul sister Brittany." Eunice closed her eyes, and with that simple act Violet and Alice felt heard. A mutual understanding of the power of found family was their truth.

"So Britt has Bess?" Eunice's concern for their car made Alice love her more.

"Britt will have Bess when all the repairs are finished," Alice said.

"I think we're going to fly to the little airport a few miles from the park," Violet explained. "We were looking through our contacts and we have a friend, Walt, who charters for climbers. We're waiting on confirmation but I'm pretty sure he'll help us."

"You think he can handle a flight on such short notice?" Eunice questioned.

"Yes, he sure will because he *really* likes Alice." Violet bumped her wife. "*Really really* likes Alice."

"Oh, that sounds quite interesting." Eunice leaned forward, resting both hands on her walking stick. "Do tell."

"You don't even know how interesting it is." Alice rubbed her blushing face. "We flew together when we were wild college kids. He thought we'd make cute babies and I thought he'd make a great flying buddy."

"He didn't know you only dated women?" Eunice angled toward the circle, grinning at Simone who was poking at the smoldering log until it caught flame again.

"He had no idea I only dated women until we picked Britt up for an excursion. It was like watching the tumblers of a lock drop into place. Once that door opened, my not-so-secret life was so obvious he smacked himself for days." Alice chuckled.

"It was all in good fun, I hope." Eunice relaxed in her chair, holding Simone's hand in her lap.

"Oh, absolutely all in good fun." Violet smiled. "Walt's married now. Got a husband. His name is Guy and they have two dogs. Guy is hilarious." She laughed. "Guy and I love to harass the two of them about the crush." She felt Alice bump her teasingly.

"Guy is a laugh-riot," Alice quipped. "He likes to harass Walt about his faulty gaydar, and I like to remind him it's different for our pansexual friend."

"Don't I know it," Simone added, pausing to watch the reaction. The smiles that followed reassured them of their safety in this family circle.

The fire popped and crackled as it consumed the pine log Violet added. Their conversation faded into comfortable silence as they watched tiny glistening sparks rise in the air.

"Auntie, if you don't mind, we'd like to stay with you for one more day and catch that ride with our friend Walt?" Violet asked.

"One more day with my favorite people sounds like the best way to celebrate night two of Solstice."

"Oh, I almost forgot." Violet jumped up from Alice's lap and ran into the house.

Eunice raised her eyebrow, questioning the sudden departure.

Alice shrugged her shoulders. “My wife, so unpredictable after all this time.”

Eunice smiled. “Keeps the spark alive.”

“Sure does,” Alice agreed.

Violet returned with a wad of material in her hand. “I can’t believe we almost forgot.” She unrolled the crumpled shirt, revealing the roller derby team logo. “Stacey sent this for you with all of her love.”

Eunice was giddy, clapping hard and rocking back and forth on her chair with delight. “This is their team shirt?” she asked, turning it so Simone could see the logo.

“That is an actual team shirt. Not something any fan can get,” Violet added.

“I’ll wear it with honor.” Eunice draped it over her chest.

The flash glared as Alice took a quick picture. She held the photo up to them. “PB is going to lose it when she sees you in her shirt.”

~~~~~~~~~~~

“I think we’re going to turn in.” Eunice stood, holding a hand to Simone. “You’ll blanket the flames?”

Violet nodded. “We’ll cover it for the night. Go get some rest. You’ve been a busy lady today.”

Eunice patted Violet’s cheek. “Blessed Yule to you, my dear.”

“Blessed Yule to you, too, Auntie.” They held eyes for a long moment, the exchange warming Violet’s heart.
~~~~~~~~~~~

"We'll see you in the morning," Eunice said as they made their way toward the house.

Alice slid a metal grate from behind the garage—the perfect size to fit the celebration circle. The two of them covered the fire pit to keep the ash inside. "Tidying the rest of the circle can wait until tomorrow," Alice said, as they walked to the house. "How are you feeling about Simone?"

"Holy shit." Violet cupped her mouth. "I can't remember the last time Aunt Eunice had a person."

Alice climbed the stairs, the aroma of their Yule celebration hanging in the air. "I think she dated someone three years ago, but definitely not a butch like them." She hitched her thumb toward the back yard.

"Makes you look femme, huh?" Violet joked.

"Not even close." Alice laughed. "I like Simone. Eunice seems happy with them."

"Yeah, she really does." Violet held a hand to her wife. "How are you feeling?" she asked as she closed the bedroom door behind them.

"I think every bump and bruise was worth it," Alice whispered. "I forget how it feels to be here. It's been twenty years, and your aunt makes me feel like she'd kill for me."

"She probably would." Violet pushed Alice against the bedroom door. With one hand pressed possessively on a muscled shoulder, Vi maneuvered the top button on her wife's shirt. "She'd pop a cap in whoever it was and cauldron the shit out of them." Her finger hooked the next few buttons on Alice's shirt.

"Pop a cap?" Alice stopped the button-hooking hand. "Who are you?"

Their palms pressed together, playfully. Violet tipped on her toes to kiss her wife. "Just a crone-in-training and right now I think I might like to join the mile high club."

Alice swallowed hard, her voice breathy as she hummed, "Umm…Vi, we're not on an airplane."

Their lips were a whisper apart. "Mile post club then." Violet pushed her wife's chin with the delicate touch of her fingertip, and moved her lips close but barely touching.

"Not on a train, either." Alice swallowed hard as teeth nipped the muscled part where her neck met her shoulder.

"Maybe, and I know there's no maybe about it, you're going to have to pretend." Her lips vibrated against the flesh of Alice's chest. "Hmm?"

"Anything you want, love. Any—thing—at—all."

# CHAPTER SIXTEEN

The water in the bathroom turned off and Alice heard her wife move from the shower into the bedroom.

"Eunice is going to harass us. I know it." Alice folded the dirty pants into her duffle bag. Her hair was still dripping from her shower, leaving spots of water on everything going into the bag. Almost fully dressed, aside from putting a flannel over her undershirt, she looked at her towel-wrapped wife. The love bite above Violet's right breast was testament to their satisfying evening.

"We've had sex in this house hundreds of times." Violet chuckled, her dimples deep with happiness and a heated flush to her cheeks. She was fresh from her solitary shower, dissatisfied by her inability to convince Alice to conserve water by showering together.

"Hundreds?" Alice questioned. "Hardly hundreds."

"Numbers, whatever. The point is she knows we do what lovers do." She slipped by her wife, intentional in the way she gripped her hips as she brushed against Alice's backside.

"Most married people don't..." Alice looked up from her bag as the gray shower towel dropped to the carpet.

Violet's grin was wicked. Satisfied with her wife's reaction, she took the flowing, floral dress from the suitcase and gave it a little shake to loosen the rainwater wrinkles. "You were about to say something heteronormative?"

"Nope." Alice's eyes raked over the naked body in front of her. "I was absolutely going to say thank you for last night." She pulled Violet into her arms. "And that I love you." Her hands rested on the curve of Vi's naked hips.

"If you don't move your hands, we'll be late for lunch."

"You mean breakfast, right?"

Violet grinned, a twinkle of mischief in her eyes. "Oh, no. I definitely meant lunch."

Alice's hands flew up like a bandit caught in the act. "I will be exiting this plane, train *and* automobile before it all goes sideways." She backed away from her wife.

Playing along with a mischievous gleam in her eyes, Violet counted the vehicle metaphors on her fingers. "Oh, my sweet burly woman. Last night you earned a point for getting us at least a mile high." She bent her index finger. "You definitely got me off the ground. Right against that door."

Barely able to say a word, Alice licked her lips and mumbled, "Mm-hmm."

"And that mile post club." Violet bent her middle finger back to count their second intimate ride. "I think I earned that trophy, right over there." She pointed at the bed.

Alice was enjoying naked amorous Violet and gladly played the game. "You absolutely gave me a gold medal, five star and blue ribbon experience all the way, baby."

"But you see—" Violet stepped forward until their bodies touched—"I'm not so sure about that automobile situation." She was standing between Alice's parted legs, in her wife's personal space, which for the last twenty years was her favorite space to invade. "I think I might like to modify that three minute, three mile rule to include a mile ride club option." The slow gulp made Violet giggle.

"Of all things, Vi." Alice's plea was throaty. "You do that any longer and Eunice is going to think we died up here."

Violet blinked, mashed a hard kiss on Alice's lips, patted her chest and took a step back. "So, late for dinner is probably off the table, too, I guess."

Alice fanned her face. "Love, the things you do to me."

"I can do them again."

In slow, deliberate motion, Violet stepped into her dress, shimmied the fabric up over her hips and slid her arms through the sleeves. It was all for her, and Alice enjoyed every second.

Violet turned around. "Wanna zip me?"

"Hell yes, I do," Alice whispered in her wife's ear. Her hand held steady as she caressed the bare skin as it disappeared behind the zipper.

"Very well done." Violet turned around, her lips inches from Alice's. "Think you can make it through the day, Handsy McHandsy?"

"Me?" Alice patted her chest. "I'm not the braless one here."

"This is cuter without it." She twirled and the skirt floated around her.

"Just for the record, I'll be thinking *underneath your dress* thoughts all day."

Violet's fingers tangled in Alice's as she opened the bedroom door. "Exactly where I want them."

The dimpled smile left Alice speechless as they paused at the top of the stairs. "I'll remember that."

"Good morning," Eunice said, looking up from the notebook she was writing in. She glanced at the clock. "Or should I say good afternoon?" There were two mugs on the table but only one had steaming coffee in it.

Violet checked her watch. "It's not even eleven yet."

"Maybe in your neck of the woods," Eunice teased, tipping her pen to point at the clock on the wall. "But around here we call it almost lunch time."

Violet hadn't looked at a clock since rolling into the train station, completely forgetting about the zone changes as they traveled into Mountain Time. "We're so sorry."

"Don't give it another thought. Solstice energy wakes the soul and rocks it back to sleep." Her cheek raised with a knowing smile and Vi wondered what mischief the woman might have created for herself last night.

"Did you have company for breakfast?" Violet asked as she picked up the nearly empty coffee cup by the sink.

Eunice sing-songed a "Maybe."

"Are you and Simone a thing?" Vi moved around the kitchen, filling a mug with coffee for herself and making one for her wife.

"A thing?" Alice repeated, and the two of them stopped to watch Eunice blush.

Eunice cleared her throat. "We are enjoying each other and that's all you need to know for now."

Alice balled a splinted fist, jokingly punching in the air as she asked, "Do I need to have a one-on-one to explain how to treat my auntie?" She winced when she flexed the sprained wrist.

"Settle down, sweetie. I think she can handle herself." Violet set the steaming mug in front of her wife.

Alice blew across the top of her coffee. "Where is Simone this morning?"

"They had to drive a friend to the train station."

"Ugh, don't say train ever again. I don't want to think about riding a train for at least a decade."

"Was it that bad, honestly?" Eunice asked. She scribbled a few notes in her book and closed the cover.

"Auntie, it would have been very romantic if it wasn't for the pack of wild children sharing the car with us."

"How unfortunate." Eunice walked across the kitchen, tucked her notebook into the cabinet over the stove, and returned with a small fabric bundle. "This is for you and for Bess." Eunice opened Alice's hand and with the most loving touch sandwiched the bundle between their palms. "When the three of you are back together, tuck this in your dashboard."

"You're blessing Bess for us?" Alice asked.

"She needs a nice restart."

"Thank you," Alice said.

Eunice walked to the back door. "Would you like to celebrate the second day of Solstice with a little bit more of that spiced wine?" She winked.

"Heck yes, we would." Violet dumped her coffee in the sink and followed her aunt out the door.

Alice sat at the table for a moment, contemplating the misadventures of the last few days, squeezing tight to the tiny, blessed bundle in her palm. Eunice was a thoughtful woman and this scented pouch was proof. Alice watched through the glass door as her wife shared a story with animated enthusiasm, counting herself lucky to know these strong women and call them her own.

# CHAPTER SEVENTEEN

"Remember to put that bundle in the dashboard." Eunice patted Alice's cheek where she'd left a bright red lipstick kiss behind.

"I'll remember." Alice wiped her face, never knowing if the woman meant to leave it there but aware that she always did.

"You take care of that wonderful wife of yours," Eunice said as she hugged Violet a little tighter. "Thank you for all of your efforts. The Yule log was perfect and our Solstice was beautiful."

"Thank you, Auntie, and I'll keep my woman perfectly safe if she'll let me." They laughed but Alice frowned as she threaded her head through the shoulder strap of her duffle bag.

"We'll see you in February." Violet hugged her one more time. They watched Eunice climb into her car, pump the gas pedal like a toddler zonked-out on sugar and rev the engine to life.

"I'll see you in February," Eunice said as she reversed out of the parking space and drove away.

"Gosh, I hope I'm that amazing at seventy," Violet said as she wiped the lipstick mark from Alice's cheek.

Alice did the same lipstick removal on Violet's cheek. "You will be. I'll make sure you are."

The small airport was light with holiday travelers as Violet walked through the automatic glass doors. Alice was in charge of the suitcase, as always.

"Where do we meet him?" Violet asked.

"Room five." Alice opened the door with Walt's name painted on the glass and stood near the windows, waiting for their friend to arrive. She studied the planes floating on the water, smiling when she noticed Walt's docked at the end of the pier.

Violet snuck up behind her wife and tipped on her toes to whisper in Alice's ear, "You know, there's something wonderful about avoiding security and not having to walk around in public with sock-covered feet while strangers dig through your luggage."

"We do tend to travel with our fair share of ding-able things," Alice joked, raising her shoulder so she could put an arm around her wife. "And that set of crampons you put in the carryon that one time? It was almost ridiculous the way it set the TSA guy off."

"Simple mistake." Violet tucked herself into Alice's arms.

"I thought they were going to drop you to the floor."

"Me too, and then you went all large with the butch." Violet relaxed against her. "So incredibly hot."

"Hey, lovebirds," Walt interrupted, and the women turned around.

"Come on, man. Can't you see we were having a moment?"

Walt's laugh was a charming greeting. "When you're done, do you think you might be ready to rock and roll?" he asked.

Alice took a second to give Walt her full attention. He was dressed casually in jeans and a white polo shirt, with an aluminum clipboard resting on his hip. When her glance fell to his feet she paused to take in his western style footwear.

She tried not to laugh as she asked, "What's with the boots, Bud—dy?"

He'd always been a hiking shoe person but he proudly kicked a foot forward, displaying his boot from heel to toe. "Pretty smart, don't you think? Guy had them made for me."

"They are something. I'm not sure smart would be my first choice," Alice joked. "He still loves you, right?"

"Shut up!" He nudged her shoulder, noticing the wrap on her wrist. "What the hell did you get into?" He turned toward the exit. They followed him through the small lobby and pushed against a door leading to the piers. Walt's bright green plane was a standout among the others as it sat bobbing on the surface of the lake.

"This?" She held up her sprained wrist. "I zigged when I should have zagged."

"Classic wrong move." He kept a straight face but Violet burst out laughing.

"You told him, didn't you?" Alice tugged her wife's hip. "Not nice, wife."

"Every climber knows…"

She pointed a finger at him. "Don't say it, buddy. If you say it, we aren't flying today. Remember I can still take you with one fist."

He held his hands up in surrender. "You got me." He escorted them down the length of the pier, the water lapping against the slatted boards in perfect rhythm with the pulsing waves. "I need to check a few things and then we fly. Get yourselves settled in. You know the routine."

Alice gave a thumbs-up and Violet waited for Walt to release the door so they could board. When they were comfortable in their seats, Violet fit her headset over her ears, keyed the mic and was satisfied she could talk during the flight.

Alice felt the weight of the headset as it covered her ears. The motion of the water around her disappeared, but the memory of the vibrational silence took her back in time. She closed her eyes, reminding herself that there was no threat to her safety on this flight home.

That wasn't the case twenty years earlier, and she struggled with the sense memory. No one was holding life together with ripped t-shirts and duct tape. The moisture in her hand was perspiration, not blood. She rubbed her palms across the fabric of her pants. Triggers weren't always, if ever, avoidable but she'd get through it.

"You alright, sweetie?" Violet's voice crackled through the headset.

Alice felt the force of her wife's love tethering her, reinforcing her place in time, in the present. "Yeah." She let out a deep sigh. "Just remembering."

Violet held her wife's hand, giving a quick squeeze of understanding. "I've got you." Her gentle touch was enough.

Alice relaxed into the present and startled when another voice interrupted.

"Ready to roll?" Walt asked, having heard their conversation but waiting for them to settle in.

Violet gave a thumbs-up for the couple, and the plane began the short taxi atop the water.

"Shouldn't be more than an hour flight time." Walt's hands flipped switches and turned dials that Violet appreciated but didn't understand.

"Sounds great," Violet said, knowing that Alice was settling herself and she'd disappear while they were in the air. Flying was always a reminder of their extraction from the cougar attack, and ultimately the reason why Bess had three-hundred-thousand miles on her odometer.

Alice wanted to love the world from an airplane, but the assault on her senses prevented it. Height wasn't the problem, whether it was on a mountain top, dangling from a cliff, or huddled in a tent tethered to a rock wall, it was her inability to act in an emergency that kept her on edge. Peeking through the window of Walt's small plane, she hoped one day it wouldn't be such a struggle. The flight was not the break from chaos she needed to recover from the last few days.

"Still good back there?" Walt's voice came through the headset.

"A-okay!" Alice gave a thumbs-up and closed her eyes. She hadn't planned to sleep and was surprised when the plane's pontoons met the lake's surface. From this point on they were mostly a boat, and Alice was content with that.

The airport building came into view, and, moments later, Walt had the plane secured to the pier.

"Not so bad, hon?" Violet asked through the headset.

Alice nodded. "Not so bad."

The door of the plane swung open and Walt held out a hand to help Alice to the pier.

"Walter, you make me less afraid of small planes," Violet said as Alice held a hand to help her out.

The waves on the lake were choppy, heaving water up through the slats of the pier, getting their feet wet. Walt was already pulling their bags, waving like a wild-child at Britt who stood leaning against the park services truck. Her feet were kicked out as if she'd been waiting hours near the end of the pier.

"Thanks, I think making passengers less afraid is a good thing," Walt joked as they walked toward shore.

"I can't say I loved the flight, but I sure like how easy you made it for us to get here." Alice hooked her arm around the man's shoulder as he gave her a grin.

"Anything for you, beautiful." He winked at Alice.

"Careful, Guy might not like you flirting with my wife," Violet teased.

"You're absolutely safe with me." He wiggled his ring finger.

Alice patted his shoulder. "Thanks for bailing us out."

They hugged tightly, and he lingered to whisper, "I'm glad everything worked out."

"Me too," Alice whispered back. "Come for dinner the next time you're in town."

"Will do." He raised a hand to wave at Britt again.

"Bring that Guy of yours, too," Violet yelled over the noise of the airplane engine revving as it landed in the water behind them.

Alice was already half-way to the waiting park ranger. Even out of uniform, Britt looked like a woman in charge.

"I wouldn't think of visiting you without him," Walt yelled as he headed down the pier and back to the plane. Guy had a schedule to keep. "Safe travels."

"Thanks, man," Alice yelled.

"Well, aren't you just the fancy-pants private jet setters?" Britt's shoulders were against the cab of the truck, her body leaning with absolute sass.

"Oh, bite me, bitch," Alice clapped back and hugged her. "That is hardly a jet. It has pontoons, for fuck's sake."

The ranger laughed as she turned to hug Violet. "Hello, beautiful."

"Hi, Britt. Thanks for the ride." They held each other for a long moment and neither wanted to be the first to let the other go.

"I'm glad it's an off day." Britt took the wheeled suitcase from Alice and carried it to the back of the truck. She turned to get a full look at her friend. "What the hell happened to you?" She poked at the splinted wrist.

"Not enough hip," Violet answered, knowing that their friend would understand immediately.

"Who has the wall?" Britt climbed into the truck laughing at the probability of her friend suffering a wrist injury on a climbing wall. Alice knew a lot about surviving in the wild, but if she was an expert at anything, it was climbing.

Violet slid in, followed by Alice who answered, "We went for a climb at PB's."

The silence that followed was a collision of emotions, each of them knowing what to say but not wanting to be the one to say it.

Britt draped her arms over the steering wheel as she turned to ask, "Uh, how is Jam-girl?" She didn't wait for the answer as she keyed the ignition to start the truck.

"She's good," Violet answered after another silence.

"So, she's climbing again?" Britt shifted the truck into gear, almost too exaggerated for the automatic transmission.

"She's got this amazing village inside a huge warehouse," Vi shared. "They built an indoor wall and..."

"How'd it feel?" Britt asked, her eyes on the road ahead, absolutely afraid of the feelings that would come if she looked at Alice.

Sweat collected on Alice's face. She rolled the window down to let the wind delay her answer.

They stopped at a red light and Britt asked again. "When you tied in?" She looked at Alice with glassy eyes. "How did it feel?"

With tears rolling down her cheeks, Alice choked out, "Like being right there again."

A car horn sounded behind them and all three noticed the green light. Britt accelerated slowly.

"Why didn't you stop?" Violet's question was a whisper.

"PB didn't need to know what was happening. Fuck, I need to climb almost as much as I need to breathe." Alice tugged at the velcro on her splint. "It doesn't happen every time, but when it does, it's hard. And I absolutely hate that the one thing I need to make me feel challenged is also the thing that breaks me into pieces."

Britt spread her palms on the steering wheel, anchoring at ten and two, revealing the wicked scar and the absence of her thumb and index finger. "I don't think you could have said it any better, Al. I need the trails out there the same way you need to tie in and dangle on a rope."

Violet reached for the scarred hand, holding tight to the woman she admired. Her head fell against Alice's shoulder, connecting them by more than the wounds of the past.

Britt didn't let go, because Violet was one of the few people in her life that didn't hesitate to touch the scars. "I love you guys, you know."

"We love you too," Alice said. "You're probably the only person besides PB that understands."

"Maybe we should see each other more often." Britt wiped her eyes with the collar of her shirt.

"I promise," Alice said, and Violet squeezed Britt's hand in agreement.

They drove for another mile before Alice couldn't stand the silence. "How's Bess?"

"Oh." She hesitated. "Bess looks really nice." She snickered. "You're gonna love what Pete did to her."

"Did to her?" Alice gripped the door handle.

"Oh, yeah." Britt made an exaggerated turn.

"My Bess better not be a fucking clown car." Alice leaned toward the dashboard to stare at her friend.

Violet held up a hand. "No one is going to desecrate your baby."

"It's so much better than a clown car. The color is kick-ass and she sounds like she could tear up the track, Harley style." Britt patted Violet's hand, signaling the harassment to come.

"Bitch, you better be bullshitting because the last few days have been about the max I can handle." Alice waved her wrist in the air. "This was just the beginning. So, tell me my girl is alright."

"Your girl is stunning." Britt smiled. "And Bess looks amazing, too."

Violet kissed Britt's cheek. "You angel. I love you so much."

Alice shook her head. "Stop flirting and tell me how she is."

Britt activated the phone mounted to the dash. "She looks like she did the day we shopped for her."

Violet held the screen out to her wife, displaying the image of Britt hugging Bess.

"You made her your home screen picture, with Pete in the background giving a thumbs-up?" Alice shook her head.

"Cute, huh?"

Violet returned the phone to the dash mount. "It looks like he did a great job."

"I checked every day. We're, like, better than besties now." Britt crossed the middle and ring fingers on her scarred hand and raised her hand to emphasize it.

"Thank you." Alice relaxed against the door of the truck. "Can you take us to the shop?"

"Nah, I can't." Britt chuckled.

"Why not?" Alice asked.

"You'll see when we get there."

Violet held her wife's hand, tucking it in her lap. "I'm pretty sure Alice has had enough adventure in the last week."

"Really?" Britt turned onto the highway in the opposite direction of Pete's shop while Violet shared the mishaps of the past few days.

"The village is what Stacey calls her place," Violet explained.

"And the climbing wall is to keep her in shape?" Britt asked.

"I think roller derby is doing that. PB uses the wall to spread the climbing love," Alice joked as she waved her splinted wrist.

"I think that's a good decision."

"So do we," Violet said.

"How was the Solstice celebration?" Britt changed the subject and Alice gave an obvious sigh of relief.

"Solstice was wonderful as always, and the extra day with my aunt was a treat."

"How is Aunt Eunice?"

"She's got a new hottie." Violet grinned.

"Seriously? A silver fox?" Britt joked.

"Absolutely. Their name is Simone and Auntie has good taste." Violet winked.

"Real—ly?"

"They're a beautiful, outgoing artist and Aunt Eunice seems very happy," Violet added.

"I miss her." Britt turned down the forestry road.

"You should come with us for Imbolc," Alice said, realizing where they were heading.

"Maybe I will. Eunice is good medicine for the soul."

"She sure is," Violet agreed.

"Here we are." Britt slowed as they approached the spot where Bess sat. The Outback was resting in the shade of the offending tree.

Alice didn't say a word as she hit the lock button and hopped out of the truck.

It was an adorable reunion to watch. Alice's finger danced across the hood, from the passenger side to the driver's. The front-end repairs were almost as beautiful as the original, with nearly perfect restoration to the dent and a glistening new headlight. The windshield and side mirror had been replaced. Alice squatted to inspect the color matching. Pete's mechanics were definitely artists. Alice's broad smile was confirmation that *her* Bess was back.

"Keys are right here." Britt tossed them to her.

Before Alice opened the door, she reached in her pocket and clipped the shiny stone back on the keyring. "I can't believe she looks so perfect."

"Thank Pete for that." Britt tucked her hands in her pockets, rocking back on her heels. "I was on him every day."

"Bess looks like her old self." Alice sat in the driver's seat, touching every element on the dash. There was no sign of broken glass, tree branch remnants or leaves of any shade. "She's beautiful."

"Here, put this in the glove box." Violet passed Aunt Eunice's blessing bundle to her wife.

"Perfect." Alice closed the door.

Violet adjusted herself in the passenger seat. "How's she sound?"

Alice started the engine. "Exactly like the day she was born."

Britt opened the driver's door to lean in. "The shop guys drove her backward as much as they could, so she's still—" She pointed at the odometer and let Alice finish the sentence.

"She's still at three hundred thousand." Alice relaxed against the headrest. "We can still get that picture."

Violet opened the door and handed her phone to Britt. "Will you take the picture for us?"

"It'd be an honor." Britt said.

"The car's in park, right?" Violet asked her wife.

Alice pushed the shifter once, and then again to double-check. "The car is most definitely in park."

# CHAPTER EIGHTEEN

The bell above the door jingled as Alice walked inside the framing shop. She didn't see an employee so she called out, "Is anyone here? Can someone help me with a project?"

Alice set the envelope on the service counter blocking her from entering the rest of the framing studio. She was standing in the only framing shop in town, a place she'd never been inside of on her own because Violet had the artist's eye.

"I can surely give it a try." A man walked around a tri-fold paper- and wood-framed dividing wall.

Alice removed the photograph from the envelope. "I'd like to frame this but I'm not sure how I want it or what I want it to look like." She turned the image around so he could take a good look. "I know I want it to be special."

The man slipped white cotton gloves on his hands before picking up the photograph. Alice was touched by the attention taken to how precious it might be. "Looks like a great bunch of friends." He looked up at her and then back at the image. "This one is you?" He pointed but didn't touch.

"Sure is." She felt a sense of pride in the moment. "A few years or twenty ago," she joked.

"Gorgeous view from the top," he said.

Alice nodded. "We had a lot of them." Looking down at the smiles in the photograph, she could appreciate the people they were and how each of them were trying to let go of what was, so that they could get to the now of their lives.

"So you're not sure how to frame it, but you want it framed?"

She shrugged. "Yes, and I'd like to hang it on my wall."

"And you want it matted?"

She shrugged again. "Yes, I think so."

"Follow me." He waved her beyond the barrier table, carrying the photograph like a precious artifact as they walked to the huge work station in the middle of the shop. The walls around them were covered with L-shaped samples of every style and color of framing material he sold in the shop. Alice was, in a single word, overwhelmed.

"I've got an idea," he said, as he laid the photo on the tabletop.

"I'm glad you do, because this is a lot." She waved at the samples on the wall.

"Framing is what I do, and I've got just the right style to highlight this memory."

They spent an hour laying samples out. As Alice shared the story behind the photograph, the man cut perfect angles in the wood and tapered the heavy matting board to fit around the photograph. He explained his life in the art world and how he came to own the small shop, declaring that he never did same-day jobs but could sense Alice's reluctance to leave the photo behind. So she was patient while he worked, and he was masterful in executing his plan.

He disappeared behind a privacy screen and Alice heard the delicate puff of an air compressor firing. Her guess was a stapler fixing the frame pieces together. Moments later, he called out from behind the screen.

"Okay, Alice, close your eyes," he said as he prepared to flip the frame around.

She thought it was silly since she'd watched him working the entire time. She placed her hands over her eyes.

"Voilà, take a look."

Her gasp was everything he needed, and a smile stretched his face.

"It's absolutely perfect," Alice said. "Can I please order another one exactly like this?"

~~~~~~~~~~~

Violet heard the lock on the front door and moments later her wife's voice. "Hi love, I'm home."

"In the living room," Violet said. "Were you able to find something?"

"Yep and believe it or not he made it while I waited." Alice kissed her wife. "I think it's perfect." She opened the bag. The framed image was wrapped in thick layers of pebble-patterned tissue paper.

"It's like a present." Violet waved her hands over the parcel.

Alice snuck her finger into the fold and tore the tape. "Just for us." The paper fell away, revealing the backside.

"The cardboard is pretty." Violet rubbed the material's surface. "And the hangers feel very secure," she teased as she tugged the wire.

"Uh huh, and the foam core is acid-free." Alice gave her a crooked grin followed by an eyebrow waggle. "It'll protect the picture from all those chemical things."

"Chemical things?" Violet giggled. "Very technical."
~~~~~~~~~~~

"I took notes." Alice held up the palm of her hand, showing her the scribbled words.

"You sure did. Do I get to see the actual framed picture?"

"Don't you want to know about the number four rubber-coated hanging wire?" Alice tucked her fingertip into the gap between the foam core and the wire.

"It's lovely. Did he let you tie the knot?"

Alice bumped her wife's hip. "Such a smart ass."

Violet opened her wife's palm to look at the rest of the scribbles. "Pebble number seven?"

"That's the frame style. I ordered one for Britt."

"She'll probably love it."

"Probably?" Alice questioned.

"Well, I haven't seen it yet so how am I supposed to know?"

Alice turned the frame over. "I think it's absolutely perfect."

"Oh." Violet reached to touch the image.

"He used museum glass," Alice said.

"Sweetheart, this is heart stopping." Violet cradled the frame in her palms.

"So you like it?"

"I like it." Violet tipped the frame. "I like it a lot."

"The shopkeeper was super nice, and when I told him the story of our Solstice travels he said I'd earned a discount even though there was a storewide sale until the first of the year," Alice explained. "So he did this." She presented a smaller frame, built from the same materials but half its size.

"You went to the right place." Violet carried the smaller picture to the living room wall.

"I think I want to hang them together," Alice said, holding up the newly-framed image of Britt, Stacey and herself. Violet held the simply-framed image of the Outback odometer with Violet and Alice smashed against the windshield. They were perfect snapshots wrapped in the fabric of time, a capsule of then and now that Alice wouldn't change if she could.

"Perfect together," Violet whispered.

Alice snaked her arm around her wife's hip. "Absolutely perfect."

Thank you for reading Yule Be Home For Solstice.

## MORE BOOKS BY SHARON K. ANGELICI

### MARK OF THE MAKER (BOOK 1 OF THE MAKER SERIES)

Wildwood Blackstone believed her dream of being a country blacksmith was coming true. When the town of Bannock hires her to restore their abandoned carriage house built in the 1800s, she can't wait to begin.

But there are more than ghosts in Bannock and shortly after her arrival she discovers this truth. When a childhood friend answers a call for help, Wildwood finds a part of her past that she longed to rediscover. Together they reveal Bannock's secret and uncover the Mark of the Maker.

## THE MAGICK AND THE MAKER (BOOK 2 OF THE MAKER SERIES)

Wildwood Blackstone longed for a life as a small-town blacksmith. She didn't imagine monsters or magick, and she never expected to fall in love with Shay.

Book two of the Maker Series finds the two women tangled together in the dark secrets buried deep in Bannock's small-town history. Is their commitment strong enough to carry them through? Who is the keeper of the Magick? When will Wildwood and Shay uncover the mystery behind the Mark of the Maker?

## THE ORIGIN OF THE MAKER (BOOK 3 OF THE MAKER SERIES)

Wildwood and her girlfriend Shay have uncovered Brigid's secret hidden deep in the earth.

Who is the stranger in the carriage house? How are they there? What do they know about the secret and the power it holds? Can Wildwood and Shay find the answers and keep fighting the monsters hunting them night and day?

## THE LEGACY OF THE MAKER (BOOK 4 OF THE MAKER SERIES)

In a secret world filled with magick, Wildwood Blackstone has encountered unbelievable mysteries. As the blacksmith in her new hometown, she's survived and endured the call to wield the hammer of the goddess Brigid, but to what end?

Celebrating a year with her girlfriend, Shay, the two continue their search for answers. What lived inside Andrea Peters? How did the entity survive for hundreds of years? Who controlled her all this time?

Their call to be The Magick and The Maker of Bannock comes with more questions than ever, but it might also come with answers to their past. Wildwood and Shay are drawn into endless realms, all of which lead to the Legacy of the Maker.

**CONNED**

For Ella Eastman, firefighting is life. She's devoted her body to being the best, but everyone needs a break from reality once in a while. For Morgan Hail, art is life, but she has to make a living. Their lives collide when television fandoms intersect at The Blacktree Comic Palooza.

Morgan's captivating fanart leads to a heated misunderstanding, and a cosplay contest brings these two women together–though only one of them knows the truth. This unlikely pair heats up when their real-world lives collide, but what will happen to their budding romance when Ella reveals her secret identity? And can they find a way to make things work when Ella's job hits a little too close to home? Conned is a story of love, loss, new beginnings, and fandom.

## DEAR KANE; WHAT I WISH WE WOULD HAVE SAID

Do the words that we say in front of our children build them up or tear them down? This short story explores the consequences of hatred and bigotry when it applies, unknowingly, to someone that you love. There's a time in every relationship when a parent must let go of the dreams they have for their child, so the child can chase what they dream to become.

## IMMORTAL HUMAN TRUTH

Immortal Human Truth is a collection of poetry written by the author as she traveled to promote her first book Dear Kane; What I wish we would have said.

Each section explores experiences with love, injustice, loss and triumph of the spirit.

## SHE BELIEVED SHE COULD

What can you do in a single day? Why haven't you done it yet? Jump out of your comfort zone and dive into life as you follow the author on her journey to achieve 365 new experiences in 365 days.

# ABOUT THE AUTHOR

Sharon K. Angelici, she/her, was born in the American Midwest, but her heart and soul belong to the mountains of Colorado.

She began writing as a child, using words to recover from trauma-induced depression. As a member of the LGBTQ+ community, she's an advocate for depression awareness and suicide prevention. In 2016 she published her first book dealing with both subjects, Dear Kane; what I wish we would have said.

Sharon is a full-time lover of life and all things Pagan and Magick. She's an artist and blacksmith, which inspired her to create her Maker series. Book one, Mark of the Maker released in 2020, Book two, The Magick and the Maker, released in 2021, Book three, Origin of the Maker released in May of 2022, and Book four, Legacy of the Maker, released in June of 2023.

www.ingramcontent.com/pod-product-compliance
Lightning Source LLC
Chambersburg PA
CBHW030610310726
48979CB00003B/641

* 9 7 8 1 7 3 7 8 1 5 8 5 3 *